THE CINDERELLA MATRIX BOOK 1

CITY OF CINDERS

KENDRAI MEEKS

Dedicated to the innovators, educators, and imagination explorers.

San Francisco

2148

ɔne

"I'll get this round of drinks. You get the second from whatever we win tonight. Whoever is still standing buys the third."

"Impossible. I can't have any winnings. I'm not entering."

Scotia slid one of the brown bottles across the barroom table. "Oh, you're entered."

Eagerness and anxiety surged through Cindira, a duality of direction with which she was all too familiar. "Scotia!"

"What? You *know* you're going to win." The redhead lifted her drink, pausing to add, "you always do."

Arguing would only make Cindira look like she was fishing for compliments. But, she couldn't hide her smile. She'd never lost in the arena.

It was that fact that made her nervous.

Even though the meek coder adopted an alias for her battles, the attention it brought was building to unsafe levels. Her father's company, Tybor, hoarded its code writers, forcing them into restrictive contracts with dizzying levels of compensation, at the cost of controlling so much of what went on in their technological lives both inside and outside company walls. One of the few benefits of being the CEO's daughter was that certain exceptions had been made where Cindira was concerned. Her personal communication device, aka her comque, wasn't monitored by Tybor security, so she avoided being geotagged. If she occasionally entered an underground hackdome, it was overlooked – as long as she was discreet.

Cindira looked about, sizing up the potential competition, noting a few repeat adversaries. The Stadium, a vaunted San Francisco hangout that didn't suffer from its misnomer of a name, strove to be anything more than a dive, serving pirate coders and closeted hackers alike. "Get Jack, jacked in, and jackpot" painted in gold letters over the bar advertised its biggest cash cows: alcohol, semi-legal jackpods, and VR tournaments. Black market cryptocurrencies provided for her entry fees and allowed Cindira to collect her earnings without a trace.

Easing into something she knew Scotia wouldn't let her back down from, Cindira sat back and nursed her drink. "Which round am I in?"

"The sixth."

"The master's round?" Forehead pressed by her splayed out hand, Cindira groaned. "I wash my hands of your fiscal irresponsibility."

Scotia cackled. "Does that mean I get to keep it all if I win?"

"No, you pressured me into being here, so usual terms apply. All losses yours, all winnings are 40% mine."

They caught up on the office gossip, waiting. Finally, the speakers hummed as the gamemaster, after seating Cindira's opponent, called out her handle. "Welcome to jackpod number four, Mistress of Cinders."

"To the victor!" Cindira tipped up her glass, hoping to empty it out and fill herself with courage, before placing it, rim down, on the table.

Across the table, Scotia mimicked the move, adding, "Whomever *she* should be."

Unlike the Ferries, the Stadium had to keep up the appearance of being a legitimate business. If you wandered in at the right time of day, their burgers and fries weren't too bad, as long as you didn't put too much thought into what meat you were actually eating. Raids, if unusual, did happen, generally with the election of a new mayor or death of a formerly prominent chiphead that led to an outcry by social reform groups. Consequently, the Stadium kept its jackpods under the bar. Literally. Storage closets on the north and south side of the joint concealed hidden staircases that descended to a dank cellar just large enough to host two devices each. The players, for obvious reasons, had come to refer to the jackpods as "the coffins."

Cindira shivered as she descended, a misty, mildewy kiss of air blowing across her forehead. "You know if we ever get trapped down here when there's a tsunami, we're both dead, right?"

"Tsunami?" Scotia scoffed. "A basement in San Francisco, and ocean levels still on the rise? I'm surprised this isn't an aquarium already. I promise, if the water starts creeping in, I'll hit the emergency shut down button on the pod and get you out of here."

8

Two ancient jackpods sat before them, each sprouting wires from its underside like weeds. "Coffin" wasn't too off a description, really. Except for the fact that the devices had transparent walls and a neural saddle that looked like an upside-down pasta drainer, the similarity couldn't be overstated. On the opposite end of the bar, her opponent would be shimmying into his saddle, and she needed to do the same.

Scotia tried to calm Cindira's nerves with levity. "All ready for you, Sleeping Beauty."

The coder grimaced as she used a small step stool to climb up into the device. "Any sign of water, right?"

"The smallest drop, and I'll eject you."

She tried to ignore the smell of sweat and trace amounts of urine that clung to the inside of the jackpod. Even though death in the vreal world didn't render physical effects in reality, the suggestion to the brain of injury was enough for the host body to react poorly sometimes. So far, Cindira had never felt that kind of fear. She always won, what would she be afraid of?

As she sat back and nodded to Scotia to close the lid, her hand felt for the power button on her right side.

Black wisps spiraled in a distant gray sky. Cindira gave herself a moment to adjust to both the weight and feel of this alien body. Her massive hands shouldn't surprise her, but platforms that forced her to embody someone so different from her true self always disorientated. She hated the cheap, catalog avatars used in underground arenas like this one, avatars coded as standardized characters without reference to the player's own concept of self.

Tybor's coders build custom-made avatars that fit their users' self-projection—true or otherwise—like a glove as they strode about The Kingdom – Tybor's true cash cow, a VR playground for the rich and famous. Cindira rarely entered The Kingdom, as busy as she was with proving herself at her job, showing that she was more than the CEO's daughter, that she was the company's best coder.

Deep breaths through her mouth acclimated Cindira's native neural processes to the faux experiences, as well as let her feel her own mass. And, God, she was massive. Two-fifty stretched out on a tall, muscular frame, weighted down with armor. Not that it would do her any good. What counted in the arena was brains, not brawn.

Around her feet lay a ramshackle collection of tools and weapons: lumber, axe blades, rope, spears, stones, swords of varying shapes and sizes… a mirror image to those that her foe would have. Straw bales formed a wall around them, both as a way to force the fight into tight quarters, and to simplify the virtual platform and speed its performance. The system read the code the player thought, stringing together the tools provided into weapons of choice. Outside of this manipulation, real world rules still held. Gravity couldn't be overwritten. Day would not become night. The dead didn't come back to life.

The one left standing at the end won, in whatever way that came to pass.

Overhead, horns blared, and within two blinks, her opponent's avatar took shape across the arena. Only by seeing her enemy could she truly see herself, for what united also divided. Each had the same goal; to conquer. The only difference, the color of their tunics. Cindira's was blue, her adversary's, orange.

"Mistress of Cinders." He didn't look at her when he spoke, instead leaning over to take up one of the staffs from his armory. "Finally, a worthy competitor."

"I didn't catch your handle."

Cindira kept her eyes fixed on him as he leaned the staff against his shoulder while testing the weight of a grapefruit-sized wedge of rock in his hand. A show, of course. Neither would forget that, even now back in the Stadium, the crowd watching on the aeroprojectors hurried to get their bets registered before one of the competitors made the first strike.

"I'm called Barrel. I'm not sure why, but that's all part of the mystique, isn't it?"

"Barrel?" She searched her memory and found it wanting. "I don't remember seeing you on any of the master boards at the Stadium."

10

"Never competed there before, but they let me into the sixth round by recommendation." He strained as he familiarized himself with the balance of his newly-coded weapon, an impressive meld of axe blade to long staff that reminded Cindira of the Grim Reaper's sickle. "Best of battle to you, Mistress."

"And to you." She returned the customary salutation moments before he ran for her at full force, the staff pulled back to his right side.

He might as well have been narrating his attack.

Barrel swung only seconds after Cindira stepped to her left, giving his axe nothing but air to rend. Speed turned against him as his center of gravity shifted. Her adversary fell to the ground in a *harrumph*, barely avoiding the bite of his own weapon.

Barrel bellowed. "Coward! Diving away from an attack."

"I stepped away from an *attempted* attack," she returned. "You think the rules are different here? They're not. *The supreme art of war is to subdue the enemy without fighting.* Was true when Sun Tzu said it thousands of years ago. It's still true now, even in a virtual arena."

In a flash, Barrel regained his feet. "Thanks for the philosophy lesson, let me give you one in anatomy."

The swing came quicker this time, so much that Cindira found it difficult to maneuver her avatar's bulk away. Barrel kept a striking distance, supplemented by a step. He was a quick learner, she'd give him that. Unlikely he'd try running at her full force again.

She needed a weapon, but the opponent lay between her armaments and herself, and only the wall of haystacks lay behind her. *Those* weren't weapons, but it didn't mean they were useless. He'd need to be closer, though.

Cindira put up her empty hands as she sidled back, drawing him by instinct in her direction. "The fight seems unfair, given that I'm unarmed." Her back hit the boundary.

"You had as much time to choose a weapon as I did." He pulled back his staff again. "Or maybe you don't know the simple code it takes to weave together wood, metal, and rope. I can teach you – for a price. *Hyuah!*"

11

Dry shafts of grass scratched her fingers as she pulled the straw bale behind to her front. Barrel's weapon anchored deep within, the curvature of the blade a disadvantage, catching the bound stack that now gained strength in its formation. With one vigorous yank, Cindira took Barrel's weapon from his hands, throwing the impaled bale to the far end of the arena.

"There." She rubbed her palms down the front of her shirt. "Now we're even again."

Red faced, Barrel guffawed. "You… cheated! The bales aren't weapons!"

"Everything here is a weapon, if you figure out a way to use it. The wall's held together by a weak repeating code, but it's easily undone. I could teach you – for a price."

"Why, you—"

His response came too suddenly for her to dodge. The force of his blow knocked Cindira from her feet. Strong, angry hands encircled her throat. Left, right, up… no direction offered solace. Maybe she had been wrong. Maybe *brawn* would win over brain.

Virtual death didn't affect the real-world body, but the mind still felt the pain. Stars burst around the edges of her vision, blackness creeping in. She might as well surrender; her dead body would only up Scotia's losses. But the movement of something on the edge of her vision drew Cindira's attention. A flash of white fur, the scurry of tiny feet. Some sort of rodent? She'd never seen one in the arena before, but then again, she'd never been pinned to the ground, moments from defeat.

The creature was gone, but it had drawn her eyes to the only thing that could save her now: the stockade of weapons she'd ignored earlier. What she wouldn't give now for one of the swords, or even an axe. If wishes were weapons, Barrel would fall down dead. But no code she knew of could make things fly through the air.

"Why won't you yield, already?" Barrel's grip clenched even tighter. "You should be dead!"

The dead did not wage war. Cindira struggled to make her muscles obey, drawing up her left hand to signal while her brain attempted to piece together the necessary lines of code that would tell the program she'd surrendered. Barrel's grin widened, but only for a scant moment. The very next, his eyes filled with terror. Suddenly his hands were off her as he backed away.

"What in the hell?"

Cindira sat up, sputtering, spinning around to follow her opponent's gaze, when she too saw it. Every weapon, every blade, every staff, even the fist-sized rocks, floated in the air, poised to strike.

She blinked, and every one of them rushed forward, streaming through the air. Cindira swallowed her scream and squeezed her eyes shut. To victor was one thing. To disseminate your opponent limb from limb was quite another.

"Jesus Christ, Cindira, get out! Get out of that, quick!"

Cindira opened her eyes, seeing not the bloody gore she'd just caused, but the hood of the jackpod lifting away.

Smoke stained the air as she sat up, looking around in confusion, trying to find the source of the heat against her face. Had the jackpod overheated? She couldn't move fast enough. Adrenaline pumping through her veins pushed her to her feet and into Scotia's hold. The redhead pulled Cindira clear as white fogged the air. A bartender bearing a fire hydrant rushed past, followed by the surly gamemaster who managed the floor.

"No winner!" He threw his hands wildly through the air. "System error! No winner! All bets void!"

The crowd groaned, some shouting that Cindira had clearly been defeated, others saying that she had been on the edge of turning the tide.

Confusion clouded Cindira's thoughts. "Scotia?"

"You heard him, system error." The redhead didn't pause, too concerned with making the door. "Weapons don't just fly through the air unless something goes wrong. Hurry up, we have to get out of here before anyone tries to claim you were cheating. I don't know who the hell this Barrel is, but he was seconds away from making a half mill off your defeat."

13

"So what? He didn't lose anything. You heard the gamemaster, all bets void."

"I don't care. A man who can throw that kind of black market crypto at the Stadium isn't someone we want knowing who we really are."

Scotia may not have been alone in her thinking. As normality reclaimed her and Cindira became more in tune with her real-world surroundings, she found herself in a stream of people heading to the exit, though that also could be because the smell of smoke filled the air.

"Glitches happen," she tried to argue, looking back over her shoulder in hopes of catching a glimpse of someone befitting the name Barrel. "I'm sure it's really not that big... of a... d—"

Her words died when she saw him: Cade Fife, staring back at her with equal doses of confusion and disbelief. What the hell was her step-brother doing at the Stadium? It wasn't the high-class, in-crowd hangout he and his twin sister Kaylie usually frequented. Stalking Scotia, maybe? It wouldn't be the first time.

Or...

Cindira came to a stark realization: her step-brother was spying on her. To what end, she didn't want to imagine, and if she should find herself in a verbal shouting match with whomever 'Barrel' was, news getting back to her step-mother and eventually her father couldn't be stopped.

Cindira felt the need to be gone ASAP, outpacing Scotia in three steps and pulling her friend insistently forward by the hand.

"You're right. Let's bolt."

⟘ꟺꓛ

Cindira Tieg observed her father's second wife from the only acceptable position: at a distance. Standing at the back of the crowd came with other benefits, though. Best of which was that no one noticed you, and the last thing she wanted today was to be noticed. Already, it felt like the secret of her narrow escape the night before had taken on mass, a bowling ball imbedded in the pit of her stomach that should make everyone gawk at her.

So far, though, so good. As Kaylie gloated at the right hand of her own mother, none of the Tybor employees in the lobby had a vantage from which to notice Cindira's angry frown. Perhaps Johanna, standing at the front, *could* have noticed, if she ever cared to lend Cindira a sympathetic eye. Sadly, the mild-mannered code writer knew the only time her step-mother gave her any consideration was when barking out commands or passive-aggressive insults.

"There was a healthy crop of candidates, both from outside and within Tybor, worthy to fill the vacant Director's position." Bold, blond, and voluptuous, Johanna also had a tongue forked in the middle, even if metaphorically. "At the end of the day, the candidate who embodied our ideals, was a proven leader, and has shown herself to be not only competent but cerebral in the broadening and emboldening of our platforms, became obvious. Yes, she is also my daughter, but Kaylie's innovation to create vreal estate within The Kingdom environment itself has led to our biggest quarterly growth of profits since we launched fifteen years ago."

Cindira became a block of ice, even as Scotia blazed next to her. Or maybe it was just the hair. Her best friend's wavy array of red locks had earned her the nickname "fireball" in their boarding school days.

Scotia leaned over, keeping her voice to a whisper. Barely. "Weren't those your ideas?"

"And my code that made them possible," Cindira replied. She wouldn't mention how her marketing plans, saved in her company e-folder until she worked up the courage to show them to her father,

15

had somehow ended up in Johanna's inbox branded with Kaylie's name.

Tybor's Executive Vice-President droned on. "Kaylie also understands that, while we still hold a dominant share of the luxury VR environment market, our competition increases not only by the day, but by the hour. We need to improve our existing products and create those that will take us into the future. The Kingdom must endure, not for its own sake, but for the sake of humanity. Never forget: it makes possible Tybor's continued and independent support of GAIA. Yes, one may be the playground of the rich and famous, but the other is the salvation of the poor and voiceless."

How dare she invoke Omala Grover's gift to humanity. There were only two things Johanna longed for: power and money, preferably other people's. If not for Cindira's father's controlling interest in the company, she was certain Tybor would have pulled its support of GAIA long ago. Even after all the good the platform had done, taking most warfare into the virtual world and curbing the destruction of both the environment and societies, Johanna thumbed her nose at its continued existence.

At least, behind closed doors. Literally. How many times, while home from boarding school on summer break, had she overhead her step-mother's condescension?

Scotia squeezed her shoulder. "Don't worry. She won't last."

"Kaylie's savvy." Cindira turned to her friend. "As long as she produces results and keeps The Kingdom growing, she'll stay in that position."

Cindira couldn't visualize the situation in which Johanna would ever fire her own daughter.

"You mean as long as she has you there to clean up her crappy code." Scotia shook her head.

No doubt about that. Over the last three years, from the moment Cindira returned from abroad and took a job at Tybor, Kaylie did as little as possible, and sloppily when she did anything. Cindira cleaned up the messy code and made it actually work. Because Kaylie was her boss, she got all the credit. Because Cindira feared the fallout of going against her step-family and upsetting her father in the process, she let her.

16

Scotia continued. "Call her out."

"What, here? In front of everyone?" Cindira shook her head. "Kaylie's the celebrity face of Tybor. I'd be doing more damage to the company than helping myself. Besides, no one except you and the Kitchen crew would believe me, and they're not going to do anything that would cost them their jobs."

"I wish you had more faith in people, starting with yourself. I still can't believe you can go into the arena like you did last night and kick serious ass, but turn belly up for the Fifes. Next time you sit down to your station, code yourself a new backbone."

"This isn't the vreal world, Scotia." Cindira's meek voice only carried to the redhead. "There, I can be whoever I want to be. Here, I'm just plain, little Cindira Tieg."

Scotia swallowed a frustrated laugh. "Just because you can't code the walls here doesn't mean you couldn't knock them down if you tried. If you keep letting Kaylie take advantage of you, you're going to make her CEO someday. You need to stand up for yourself. Doctor's orders."

"I'm not sure having a PhD in social work qualifies you to..."

"It does." Her friend cut her off, and probably would have launched into her boilerplate synopsis of how Cindira's so-called family needed the intervention of one with her specific qualifications, if the man who pulled to within a few feet of Johanna didn't swipe away both of their gazes. "Shut the front door, who is *that*?"

The stranger stood out, and not just because he was handsome. Such men were a dime a dozen, given Tybor's affluent clientele and the ease of synth surgery for those of means. His face had a certain level of imperfection that suggested he hadn't been altered. One eyebrow arced a few degrees higher, a tiny bump on the side of his nose kept him from the type of unnatural symmetry the altered had.

Like Kaylie, for example.

Yes, handsome, but his presence still made her wary. Cindira took note of a silver band around his wrist. An antique watch? Since the proliferation of comques a generation before, the analog timepieces had all but died out. Unlike his face, his attire appeared engineered. Not dressed in a way to grab attention, but an effort to

CITY OF CINDERS - THE CINDERELLA MATRIX #1

avoid it. With his slate-colored suit, pressed white shirt, black leather belt, and solid black tie, he'd mastered a monochrome palate. The scheme had backfired on him at Tybor, where employees were encouraged to dress in the bright, flashy styles of the social elite to give clients the impression that they were "not only welcome to join The Kingdom, but already part of it."

This man had the appearance of someone who came from money but wanted to hide it. The way he stood at the front of the lobby, but off to the side, almost as if he needed to keep a line of sight on Johanna and the employees milling about but not be near neither suggested a tactical assessment on his part.

"Is he a member of the board?" Scotia took half a step forward, vying for a better view. "He looks so familiar."

Cindira shook her head. "I know the board members."

Scotia's overly-freckled nose wrinkled. "I know I've seen him somewhere before, but I'm terrible with faces. Trust me, *that* is not a face I'd want to forget on purpose. I wish I had your sharp memory."

"No, you don't. It's a blessing to be able to forget things easily."

The awkward level inched up as Scotia rode out the subtext. In their silence, they refocused on the tail end of Johanna's speech.

"...and I know you'll all join me now in officially congratulating Miss Fife on her new position."

A polite round of applause, short lived, tapered off. The lobby began to empty, each of the workgroups flowing towards their area of the tower. Cindira knew she needed to get back to her workstation in the Kitchens—a new batch of specialization orders had come in and she'd be coding till doomsday—but something about the way the curious man lingered forced her to do the same. She'd stay until she couldn't avoid being noticed.

"Cindira?"

She gave Scotia's elbow a little tap. "You, um... go ahead. Even if she's evil, she's still family. I should say something, or Johanna will make sure my dad knows how rude I was."

"You know what I think of that, right? But whatever, you're

a big girl. I, however, have to go." Scotia leaned in closer to Cindira's ear under the guise of trying to hug her friend. "In prison, this would be where I shove the shank into your pocket so you could take care of her."

"Love you, too."

Luckily, Kaylie's inner fandom, a hobnobbed collection of sycophantic residue feeding off each other's counterfeit glee, flanked the rising star, giving Cindira a shield of invisibility as she crept up to the edge of the gaggle.

"Oh, Kaylie!" One of them squealed, positively shaking with glee as she presented a hand. "Department Head! What an honor."

"It is," was her snide, curt reply. The soft-skinned hand drew back as soon as it could be done without looking like a snap as she examined her nails and added, "Isn't mine the position that Omala Grover once held?"

Johanna's hands clawed her daughter's shoulders as she snaked her arms around her. "Don't be silly, dear. I have Omala's old position."

As she was both the Executive Vice-President of Tybor, and Rex Tieg's wife, Cindira couldn't be sure which of the two Johanna currently laid claim to. Neither sat well.

Cade whittled himself from the crowd, pushing forward in an effort to get to his sister's side. Kaylie's twin was gray where she was bright, almost as if he'd grown pale living in her shadow. Cindira remembered having that thought the first time they'd met as children, in a time when she'd give herself over to fantasy and poetry about the wonders of the world. Kaylie was the sun, and Cade, silver moonlight. Hauntingly handsome in his own way but given to silence and sulking. Cindira had once pictured the twins in the womb looking like some sort of infantile yin-yang. He'd never been as hostile to her as the two women had, but there was a bit of sinister in his silence. Cindira suspected his motives–especially as she'd grown into womanhood. Forget the fact that they'd been step-siblings since she was nine and he, fifteen. Much worse went on inside The Kingdom, she'd heard.

He paused on the outer orbits when he saw her, smiling and laying a hand on her shoulder. "Cindy."

"Cade."

A world lay between what she wished she could say and what her tongue would agree to. *Did you see me last night? What were you doing there? Were you spying? For my father, or your mother?* But this was hardly the place to discuss such things. Cade might have even more wiggle room in his life outside of Tybor than she did, but neither had anything to gain by others knowing they'd been at the same hackdome the night before.

Instead, he veered off into an appearance of polite conversation. "I thought you'd be taking some time off. Aren't you overdue for a vacation?"

"Trying to get rid of me?"

His smug smile faltered at the veiled jab.

Cindira continued, "I'd need my supervisor's permission to take any time off. Not likely to happen anytime soon. The Kingdom is a demanding master."

Perhaps drawn by her son's gravity, Johanna had made her way to them from behind without either noticing. The snake showed just the tips of her fangs. "Greatness comes at great sacrifices."

It wasn't any less true just because Johanna had been the one to say it, and Cindira knew from experience just how much Tybor's creation expected on the altar.

"Indeed." Cindira shifted gears, driving away from the fact that Tybor's success had come on the back of her mother's legacy. "I was going to offer my congratulations to Kaylie, but I don't think her fan club is willing to give her up quite yet."

"Yes, well..." Johanna wrapped an arm around Cindira, pulling her into the fold. Such family intimacy was a move her step-mother executed whenever eager eyes were about; employee morale had been suffering before Cindira's arrival at Tybor three years ago, and the illusion of a big, happy family leading the company proved a successful cure. Besides, Johanna wasn't about to miss a chance for her step-daughter to genuflect at the feet of her own flesh and blood. "...it is difficult to get the attention of powerful people. Kaylie? Kaylie, come here, please. You see, dear, you just have to--"

"*Ah-hmm...*"

All blinked in surprise at the sound of someone clearing his throat, though Johanna regained her composure the fastest. Cindira managed to shuffle behind Johanna as they turned, but she could still see the particulars. It was him, the man that she and Scotia had noticed. He stood on the edge of their small gathering, his eyes intent but his body retracted, as though asking for permission to join them while daring any of them to deny him. His face would be the vision of any grand sculptor. Up close, Cindira could see a scarred line through his right eyebrow and the slight curvature of his nose that might be a healed injury of another sort. He became aware of her just as her gaze drifted to his gray eyes. The man looked at her, through her, beyond her, as though she were a work of art and he was trying to study her brush strokes. So briefly, and with such intensity that, even without reason, she began to feel like she was guilty of something.

When he turned his gaze back to Johanna, Cindira took the opportunity to melt back further, while still being careful to remain within earshot. She looked down at the comque on her wrist, making an effort to appear consumed in some message or task.

"Officer Batista." Johanna pulled another tissue smile onto her face, a countenance utilitarian and quickly disposed of when finished. "May I introduce you to my family?"

Cindira's stomach bottomed out as Johanna said, "My daughter..."

A moment later, from the corner of Johanna's eye, Kaylie bounced into view—far too enthusiastic to be natural. No, this introduction had been anticipated, and Kaylie acted nervous as though she'd missed her cue. Only a blind man would miss the way Johanna pushed her blond-haired, brown-eyed progeny forward, as though her daughter was the last line of protection between herself and this strange man. Kaylie presented a candied vision that could tempt a man's sweet tooth and distract him from the meat of a situation.

"And my son, Cade."

Nevertheless, he was Johanna's progeny, and well versed in civil engagement. Cade stepped forward, offering the officer a hand and quick nod of recognition. Meanwhile, Cindira waited to see if she would be acknowledged. When she wasn't, it came more as a relief than a surprise. She should take this opportunity to turn on heel and flee, but then the man spoke, and her feet refused to move.

"Thank you for allowing me to visit today. It's such an honor to see where Omala Grover made history."

His voice arrested her. She'd heard it before... somewhere? The scent of memories drifted on the breeze and shooed away. *Cedar and myrtle, and the sound of ocean waves and screaming gulls...* So much for the perfect memory all her fellow code writers credited her with. This man's voice triggered a tripwire of recollection, and explosion of the past that refused to gain clarity in the lifting smoke. She *knew* him. Only, she didn't.

"Kaylie?" Johanna's tenuous mezzo brought Cindira back to the moment. "I promised Office Batista a tour of the Kitchens. Perhaps you'd be willing to show him around?"

"Of course. It would be my *pleasure*."

Kaylie put a lilt in her voice that imbued every word with a slight hint of innuendo. Was there a mission decreed by her mother, or did she just want to bed Batista on the merits of his own physical appeal? At least there, Cindira couldn't blame her step-sister's train of thought.

Officer Batista grinned. "My father was one of the representatives to the first GAIA Congress, and he often told me that that was where the magic behind Tybor's platforms really happened. I've been curious to see it for some time."

He spoke of his father in the past tense, something that didn't escape Cindira's notice.

He continued. "That's where Omala Grover once worked, isn't it? It would be thrilling to see the place where the world was saved from the brink of destruction."

"Hyperbole doesn't suit you," Johanna laughed. "All Omala did was build the stage where the players could act."

"She did much more than that. *Much* more. It's a place where men and women can work out their differences through either diplomacy or warfare, without all the horrific real-world consequences. The thought of countries still going to war – actual war – in real life...the casualties, the damage to our planet..." Batista looked down as if to compose himself. His focus drifted from the women to the watch on his wrist. "If not for GAIA, how much more would we have lost? How much more would I—"

Something shifted in the air, and suddenly, Johanna's sacrificial lamb needed to be pushed toward the knife more insistently. "Officer Batista—"

His attention snapped back. "It's *Detective*, actually," he corrected.

A detective wanting to learn about The Kingdom? Even Cindira's own protective instincts flared at that notion. Raising any concern would only cause more problems and draw Johanna's ire, however.

"Apologies, Detective," Johanna bowed her head. "If you wanted an overview of The Kingdom architecture, it might be more effective to discuss that in Kaylie's office. The Kitchen is nothing more than a roomful of computer stations and code writers, none of whom are particularly good conversationalists."

"No, I'm very intent on seeing it." His smile was the kind born of pride, where the corners of the mouth draw back instead of up. "It's the whole reason I'm here. I hope you understand."

"Of course, it's no trouble. I'd be happy to give the *detective* a peak." Kaylie drew her arm through the air, motioning to the elevators, even as Cindira studied the flinch of Johanna's face from the lilt Kaylie gave the word *detective*. "After all, the place where we cook up all the code is really the heart of the company."

Batista cleared his throat and mimicked Kaylie's gesture, hooking his arm to hers. "Let's to it, then, Miss Fife."

"To the elevators. We have to go down to the sixteenth floor." To say Kaylie looked like a fisherman dangling his big catch to the remaining members of her inner circle as she walked by would be underselling the arrogance. Who was this man that she felt like she had to lord the fact they were so close over her fangirls? Was it just because he was someone she hadn't yet slept with? "If you'd like to follow me, I can—"

"*Eek!*"

Detective Batista's hand gripped the holster at his side as one of Kaylie's lingering retinue cried out. Everyone wheeled about on the hooked nose woman of small stature and large bosoms cowered behind a potted plant.

23

Johanna swooped about, clicking both heels and her fingers. "Jesus Christ, what was that for?"

Perhaps the woman had begun to understand the comedy of her overreaction as she squeaked out, "A mouse just ran out of the elevator."

The confidence inside Cindira imploded. She drew back into herself, both literally and figuratively. A mouse? Way up here on the twenty-third floor? How did that happen?

Batista grinned as his stance relaxed. He again offered up his arm to Kaylie. "Don't worry, Miss Fife. I'm trained in many forms of defense. I'm sure one of them works on rodents."

three

Cindira arrived in the Kitchen via the stairs just moments before Batista and Kaylie. She saw a dozen sets of eyes perk up from behind each bank of monitors when the detective stepped off the elevator. In contrast to the curious stares, Batista surveyed the Kitchen with the kind of detachment and disinterest usually reserved for convenience store deli counters. He took in each station in turn. At intervals of five feet a desk set up that included three monitors arranged side-by-side-by-side, a keyboard, a box of prototyping supplies, a mishmash of personal effects, and a code writer. A cylindrical cell that ran from floor to ceiling served as a central feature of the room, all workstations positioned to face it. *Like a Victorian surgery theater*, one of the coders had once remarked.

Batista's eyes lingered on each person for a moment, as though he were validating them against a checklist. When he got to Cindira, she turned to her screens, even as her cheeks heated. Hopefully her light olive skin masked it, though she could have sworn his eyes stayed on her a little longer than the others, as though categorizing her took extra effort.

Gone was the flirting he'd briefly displayed upstairs. The detective laced his hands behind his back and became the very model of professionalism. "Don't you use aural interfaces? Are they actually typing into keyboards?"

When had the façade dropped? In the elevator, perhaps? Cindira wouldn't put it past her step-sister to make a move along the way, triggering a less agreeable man to withdraw. She'd done as much even when Cindira had been with her. She and Scotia still used the term "express lift" as a jaded euphemism.

The cadence of keying slowed from a fierce squall to a gentle passing shower. Jeffrey Mackey in particular caught Cindira's eye, pointing while he mouthed the words, *who the hell is that?* Cindira shrugged, taking shelter in her trench of a computer station and hoping she could still hear clearly across the distance. Luckily, Kaylie chose Mackey's station for whatever show-and-tell she had planned, placing the couple right behind where Cindira worked.

"There's an AI assistant on standby, but believe it or not, the code writers prefer it." Kaylie paused, leaning over Mackey's workspace, pointing to the left-hand display filled with symbols, letters, and numbers. "Aural interfaces require natural speech. The Kingdom's supplemental code is all written in Purusha+. The code writers say it's quicker to input this way."

"It *is* quicker." Mackey's hands froze over the keyboard, the stream of key strikes ceasing with an audience watching. Suddenly, his hands went to his screen, spreading his fingers out wide to block as much of the view as possible. "I'm sorry, but this is a user's private information. It's not open for external review. Not unless you have a warrant."

Batista grimaced. This was a man who wasn't used to being told no and hadn't had a lot of opportunity in letting it go when he couldn't. As though the detective realized others might be reading his social cues, he unbuttoned his jacket and cleared his throat before resuming a nonchalant attitude.

"It wasn't my intention to pry. My apologies." He turned back to Kaylie. "Purusha+?"

"It's the language Omala Grover invented that GAIA is built on."

At the mention of her mother's name, Cindira perked up. She almost stood. *Almost.*

"I know what Purusha is," the detective continued, "but I thought it was something only its creator knew."

Kaylie backed against one of the walls, using it to arch her chest out in such a subtle way, you'd have to know her tendencies to read her distracting devices. "I know that's what everyone says, but it's not entirely true. We've been able to ferret out enough of the language through the years to keep both The Kingdom and GAIA going. Grover might have thought she was doing something no one else was capable of, but we estimate we've been able to recover about ninety-percent of it. Parusha+ is more of a derivative, really. No one will ever be able to do *everything* she did, but we know enough."

"A gap of ten percent of a language sounds pretty significant, Miss Fife." He turned his intense scrutiny on the coders with a slow sweep of his head. Cindira took eyes to her screen in desperation to remain invisible. "No one knows it all? Are you sure about that?"

"Yes." Her eyes narrowed. "Exactly what is it that you're investigating, Detective?"

Batista hesitated, his eyes filled with equations meant to measure Kaylie. Finally, he gave one miniscule nod and continued. "I'm investigating some recent developments which has us curious about the source code. I'm here representing GAIA Security. I'm afraid that's all I'm at liberty to discuss."

GAIA security? Cindira's fingers went to her throat, stroking a thumb over the indent in flesh.

Kaylie continued, "I thought security officers were permajacked into GAIA?"

"*You* must know that's just a rumor. If we stayed permajacked, our bodies would atrophy, like a chiphead's." He held out his arms, inviting her to inspect his person as evidence. "As you can see, I'm not in any kind of diminished state."

No, he is not.

"Fair enough. But still, why would GAIA want to know about the architecture of The Kingdom? The source code should be more or less the same."

"So the theory goes." Any trace of gaiety drained from his features as he held up a hand and traced a finger down the wall, drawing an invisible line that used the contours of Kaylie's body as a guide. "Miss Fife, have you noticed any subtle changes inside The Kingdom environment that you've found difficult to explain lately?"

"That's difficult to answer, Detective. It's constantly changing. The fashions, the color palates, the clientele. It might be a vreal world based on a romanticized recreation of baroque opulence, but we still have to keep its visual appeal tracking in parallel to contemporary twenty-second century tastes."

The detective began to read fluently in Kaylie's language. He leaned in, flattening his hand against the wall, just right of her forehead. Cindira should have been used to the way that men threw themselves at her step-sister. Not that Kaylie made herself a difficult catch as long as the man pursuing had the body, money, connection, status, power, and/or secrets to make him worth her time.

Cindira grabbed her mug, faking a need to top off her coffee, to position herself close enough to hear.

"Rumor is, most of those fashions change because of the styles *you* yourself debut." He traced a finger over Kaylie's bottom lip. "You're quite the trendsetter, aren't you? But where do you get all your personal things designed? Rumor is, no one can code their equal."

"I'm afraid I don't share that information. If everyone knew who my designer was, she'd jack her prices sky high and never have time for me."

Rolling her eyes wasn't a choice, it was a form of therapy. Cindira bit the inside of her mouth. *Jack her prices up.* Had Kaylie ever paid Cindira a single credit for the hundreds of hours of labor she'd done? No. The reward, she'd said, was in building a portfolio. The mystery of the unknown designer would only add to intrigue, and one day, when Kaylie was ready to share her, she would. Three years of promises had built up quite a debt, one which Kaylie was in danger of defaulting on.

Batista leaned in, his lips inches from Kaylie's. *Cheese biscuits,* the detective was as bad as her step-sister. It wasn't just Cindira gawking now. Not a single keystroke or mouse click could be heard.

"Can I at least see underneath?" He closed his eyes, as though he meant to kiss her, but didn't actually move a single bit. "Let me see the code?"

Though the two lust birds remained unaware, everyone else in the room turned on Cindira as slammed her mug on the table next to the coffee pot. *Hell. No.* She'd be damned if anyone was going to take a peek at *her* code. Not even Kaylie was allowed to see, not that she'd expressed any interest. Cindira hadn't spent years fighting off hackers for some hot lips GAIA detective to swoop in and steal her designs.

Luckily, Kaylie backed her up for once—

"I'm sorry, but without a warrant or a direct order from my father..."

—even if she did so while claiming Cindira's dad as her own.

"...no one is allowed to see *any* code. Even the coders in this room have to grant each other permission to see their own work."

28

Just as Kaylie got tired of waiting and leaned in, Batista swiveled, pulling away. "What did you mean when you said you're coding in a derivative of Purusha?" The indifference had crept back into the detective's voice. "The Kingdom has expanded since Omala Grover died fifteen years ago. How can you keep building if you don't have the full code set?"

Kaylie blinked away the confusion. She wasn't dumb; the quick switch made it all too clear Batista was attempting to play her. The only way to lose in this moment was either to renew her seductive taunts, or to appear hurt.

Even if she might be.

"What we do here is mostly cosmetic," the blonde said plainly. "We can create buildings, design avatars—that kind of stuff. But we can't figure out how the wind blows or why gravity still is present. Did you know that every snowflake that falls in The Kingdom or GAIA is unique? The code that actually lets The Kingdom function is restricted."

"Restricted from whom?"

"Restricted from everyone."

Cindira couldn't stop the half-grin that blossomed onto her face. *Not everyone*.

Kaylie continued, "The Kingdom's source code was directly copied from GAIA, and since GAIA's source code was also only accessible by Omala Grover..."

The detective balanced his chin on his balled-up hand. "Miss Fife, are you telling me that even Tybor doesn't know *how* The Kingdom works?"

"No one has ever known. Except Omala Grover, and the dead don't talk."

He stepped forward, dropping his hand and his indifference. "If you were called on by the GAIA High Court, is that something you'd attest to?"

The High Court only dealt with high international crimes. What in the hell was going on inside a hedonistic and frivolous world like The Kingdom that was being investigated with the same intensity as a war crime?

Kaylie swallowed. "Are you threatening me, Detective?"

"Not you." Batista reached up, vanity beaming from his smug smile. "Thank you for the tour, Miss Fife. It was very illuminating."

Four

Fog, as welcome as it was rare, cloaked Cindira's weary sojourn home. On nights like these, when the Kitchens kept baking code until after dark in response to some high roller's request, she longed most for the home she once shared with her mother. It still peeved Cindira that she hadn't been allowed to stay. *Can't happen,* her father had said a few days after the funeral when she'd suggested her nanny would be happy to stay on. *You just lost your mom, kiddo. I know it hurts to leave, but you need to be with family. An eleven year-old can't live without a parent, and a nanny isn't really a parent.*

A thought she almost found comforting, until the next fall when she was shipped off to boarding school. By that time, however, it seemed the lesser of two evils. Kaylie and Cade vacillated between indifference and intolerance where she was concerned. Five years their junior, their interests and concerns didn't often overlap. Johanna in the meantime barely acknowledged Cindira's presence, other than to occasionally reference her in the background of a conversation, during which she was customarily labelled either "Rex's kid" or "*that* woman's child." Exceptions proved the rule, and on the rare occasion when her parentage wowed a guest, she was forced to doll up and parade through the room as "the great Omala Grover's daughter." It didn't hurt that, other than having her father's green eyes and somewhat fairer skin, she bore some resemblance to her late mother. Johanna fawned with faux pride and sympathy, as though she were a saint who'd adopted an orphaned princess.

Cindira paused at the entry to her father's home—or, more appropriately, to the path that led to the guesthouse in the backyard—taking off her ventilator and stuffing it into her bag. City air had been predicted to clear up enough for long-term exposure two years ago. When the fog locked in the pollutants of the day, however, it was still a good idea to switch to filtered. If it weren't for GAIA, the ventilator might be a permanent necessity.

As her eyes tracked up from her side bag, a flash of white scurried across her path, making Cindira jump back and muffle a shout. Her hands tightened into fists as she chided herself. "Damn it, Cindira, it's a mouse, not a python."
31

Not that she'd care to run into one of those, either.

The gate protested with an eerie *creeeaaak*. Beyond it, an elderly woman with a mop of gray hair floating atop a nightshirt wielded a rake.

"Stop or else."

Cindira let the gate close behind her before crossing her arms over her chest. "Or else what, Auntie?"

"Auntie?" The gardening tool lowered as another arm came up to sweep away a hairline and expose the wrinkle-wrecked face of Asla Duncan. "Oh, Cindira! Cindira dear! I'm sorry. I just thought... I—"

"You were defending the house against thieves, thugs, and possibly, thespians. Yes, I know." Cindira dropped her bag at her side and divested her one-time nanny of the rake, setting it aside. "But as you can see, it's just me, as usual. You know that no one else comes in the back gate but the two of us."

Asla's eyes fluttered. "Not true. Why, I woke up from my nap this afternoon someone was poking around."

Cindira took up her bag. "Did you draw blood?"

"Ah! You make jokes. You never see the danger coming."

Cindira hooked her arm in the old woman's and walked her toward the guesthouse they shared. While she may not have her father's oppressive wealth, her mother had left her with an inheritance suitable that she could afford her own place. Only, Cindira refused to employ the woman she considered the closest thing to a mother she had on principle, and Asla, ever proud, refused not to work. The guesthouse location allowed Cindira some measure of separation from the rest of her family and gave Asla a way to keep working despite the challenges time presented for her mobility. Though if Asla ever found out it was Cindira and not the rest of the family paying her salary, all her efforts would be for nothing.

The arrangement also let Cindira prevent situations where Asla would kill someone with her frightening ninja broom skills. Ever since the night when Omala Grover had died, the former nanny saw monsters everywhere. For fifteen years, every doctor was a conspirator, every driver an assassin. She refused to accept the truth; Omala's death was nothing more than a tragic accident. Cindira's mother had slipped off the dock on a foggy, damp night and was hit by the very boat coming to pick her up. It could happen to anyone. It *had* happened to Omala.

Cindira decided to focus Asla's attention to the remaining question. "So who was it then?"

"Who was—Oh, some sort of delivery. A box with your name on it. I didn't open it."

"Did the package have a return address?"

"No, it wasn't post. Is there even post anymore? A courier from Tybor came. I thought he meant to bring it to the main house for the family, but he swore it was for you."

"Why would Tybor go to the expense of sending something here, when they could just drop it to me at the office?"

"He didn't say. Just a quick 'Is this where Cindira Tieg lives?' and that was it."

The guesthouse Cindira shared with the aging woman had originally been built as a pool house, a hundred years before. During the worst of the droughts that had come when Cindira was a baby, outdoor pools up and down the west coast were outlawed and forcibly filled. Only the outline of the former feature remained, creating a buffer between them and the main house. Now that Asla had been assured that it was only Cindira at the gate and not a thespian, she shuffled off to bed, leaving the younger woman alone with some reheated chapati, some shepherd's pie, and a box without an obvious way to open it.

As she turned it over in her hands, rotating it, looking for a seam, Cindira's imagination took off. Could it be a cake? A firesafe with a trove of money? A human head? Hopefully not that last one, though honestly, she wouldn't be interested in finding a head of *any* kind. Curiosity burned, even as reality frustrated. There was no key hole, no crease, but it wasn't empty. Every time the axis changed something moved within.

She'd have to follow up in the morning with the office, figure out who had dispatched the cube to her home, and why. For the moment, she wanted nothing more than a hot shower and cool drink—

33

Knock, knock, knock.

—Which would have to wait.

Kaylie was a woman born both annoyed and annoying. The moment Cindira opened the door, she plowed past and spun around, fists on hips. Why Asla was so scared of actors, but evil-step-siblings-turned-bosses didn't force her running into the room with broomstick in hand, Cindira couldn't say.

"I need a new dress."

"Please, make yourself at home," Cindira deadpanned, closing the door behind her step-sister.

A shaky voice called from behind a closed door. "Is it a thespian, dear?"

"No, Ms. Asla, it's only me, Kaylie," Kaylie called out over Cindira's shoulder before adding under her breath, *"crazy old bat."*

Cindira closed her eyes and huffed her frustration. She'd lecture Kaylie—*again*—about respecting the elderly, if she thought it would do any good. At least Kaylie rarely said anything rude directly to Asla's face. What Cindira wouldn't give for the same consideration.

"Kaylie, I just got home. *Just.* And as I've told you ten times before, I can't design something that complex from here. Security protocols won't let me—"

The blonde interrupted, "I know, tap into the network from a location outside of HQ or an approved satellite office. But you don't understand. I *need* it. There's a ball tonight, and I just found out Maeve Connor copied the design—by the way, what the hell? Don't you have my designs copyrighted? — and is wearing it *specifically* to make me look stupid."

Not sure she needs to go to such lengths. "I *do* have your designs—" *My designs.* "—registered, but that doesn't stop someone from making a pretty close knockoff. You know that. And I was just about to—"

"Hold on a second." Kaylie's hand traced an ominous arc, pointing to the table. "What. Is. *That.*"

Cindira didn't have a chance to conjure fresh annoyance at being interrupted yet again. Instead, she followed her step-sister's eyes, to where the mysterious box had been left for later inspection.

"That? It's nothing." Cindira's head quirked to the side as she took in the baffling sight. Not only had the box magically grown a lid; it was open.

"I know what that is." Kaylie managed to cross the room before Cindira could create an excuse to call her off.

"You do?"

"Yes, only... What the hell? Cindy, what are these?"

As Kaylie reached into the box and pulled out the contents, Cindira found herself asking the same question. At first glance, it appeared to be some sort of bowl or figurine. Whatever it was, it was mostly transparent. Only by relaxing her eyes and *not* focusing on it did Cindira come to understand the object balanced on the end of Kaylie's finger was a shoe.

A *glass* shoe.

Her step-sister laughed. "Somebody sure punked you good."

"They did?"

"Yes, they did." One corner of Kaylie's mouth rose in a lopsided smirk. She palmed the shoe for just a moment before tossing it across the room. Cindira shifted – managing to snatch it from a certain cracked fate – and landed on the couch with her hair lashed across her fate. "I saw a prototype of this last year in Bangalore. It's supposed to be a docking station for mobile jacking."

Cindira blew a raspberry. "Mobile jacking? It's a myth, not to mention, impossible. The energy and bandwidth required just won't allow for it. Even if they were real, the last thing I'd shape it as would be a glass shoe."

Product design wasn't Cindira's specialty, but it didn't take a genius to figure out the materials didn't adapt well to a form worn on the feet and crushed to the street.

"The guy in India only had the base. He had schematics for the wearable he said he'd designed for it, shaped like – get this – a crown." Kaylie picked up the box, turning it. A *swish-clunk-clunk* as she did so suggested the sister shoe lay within. "Flattery will get you a lot of places, but not into our product portfolio. This is probably something like that. People have been trying to design them for years, but like you said, it's just not possible. Anyways, as I was saying: dress."

"I can't. I'd have to go back to Tybor to—"

But Kaylie was already heading toward the door. "Don't forget, I'm your boss now. That can be a good thing, or a very bad thing for you."

"I could quit, you know." Cindira crossed her arms as Kaylie paused at the door. "Lots of other places would love to have me. Tangentry would *love* it."

Kaylie paused to turn. "We both know you'd never leave the company your parents built from the ground up. What would Omala Grover say if she found out her only daughter went to work for the competition? The dress: in my Kingdom closet ASAP. Don't forget shoes, necklaces, etc."

"Fine, but I can't design one from scratch *that* quickly. All I could do would be to modify."

"Whatever. Just make it different enough to piss off Maeve and teach her a lesson about trying to copy me."

ſiᴜe

By the time Cindira arrived back at the office, only the night guards and a few people in the complimentary customer service suite were still in the building. The former knew Cindira on sight and didn't bother to ask why she was at work at this time of night; it wasn't Kaylie's first time being a diva. The latter were jacked into the vreal world and weren't even aware of her existence as she passed their offices.

Cindira threw down her bag on her desk and called up the Kitchen's AI assistant.

Pele's soft feminine voice filled the space. "Good evening, Miss Tieg. How may I be of service?"

"I'm here by myself." *Again.* "I'm going to need help running the ops while I work inside the simulator. Open a port into The Kingdom and take me to Kaylie's room."

In the center of the Kitchens, the cylindrical chamber, some five feet in diameter, called the Sink served as both their sandbox when developing new elements for the vreal world, as well as a semi-jacked environment where products already deployed into The Kingdom could be tweaked without taking them completely offline. Cindira stepped into the chamber, a small thrill running up her spine as the tangible-light diodes, or TLDs, embedded in the floor, ceiling, and walls fired up.

Pastoral landscapes whisked by, the image dodging people—other clients inside the environment—panning over cobble-stoned streets and around the VAPORs until, at last, it reached the front of her family's Kingdom residence, Alsace. Styled after a picture Kaylie had once seen of a baroque French chateau, the two-story brick home with narrow turrets on its left and right flanks looked out of place in the heart of The Kingdom's urban center, with its rows of grand townhouses pushing out from either side. Cindira knew Kaylie hadn't been happy about its humble scale; it could barely sleep ten. For once, Johanna had put her foot down on her own daughter's vanity for the reason that ever motivated her beyond spoiling her

37

CITY OF CINDERS - THE CINDERELLA MATRIX #1

children: money. The profits to be made from the lots closest to the markets and the palace district were far too lucrative to waste on self-indulgence, even of her children.

Pele's voice filtered through a speaker above. "Authorization required to enter. Please state passcode for user *Kitchen316* to enter the premises of *Her Majesty, Queen Johanna Tieg*."

Cindira's fingers flexed and tightened as a wave of disgust curdled her insides, both because of her password, and for the reminder that her step-mother had done one old-fashioned thing by taking her father's name when they'd been married. "Cinderella."

The image dove forward again, through the front door, past the luxe entryway and the chandelier overhead, up the stairs, and into Kaylie's private suite. Once the image settled inside Kaylie's room and in front of her wardrobe, Cindira set about her work.

The microscopic sensors embedded the glass around her read each movement, translating *real* world actions into *vreal* world manipulations. Though she knew there was no actual brass handle within her grasp, Cindira's mind created faux sensations, telling her that she indeed held something. The wardrobe the length of a king-sized bed held gowns. Dozens of them in a rainbow of colors and a caravan of materials. Clients made certain agreements when they paid to play inside this virtual landscape, one being that, in order to maintain the esthetic of the fairytale world, they must dress appropriately. For women, this meant complex layers of petticoats, chemises and corsets – all designed and sold for a tidy profit by trendy designers. But even the most talented of the dress designers in New York or Hong Kong couldn't do what Cindira could with code. Kaylie might not know the extent to which her step-sister could read and rewrite this world without equal, but she knew that none other matched Cindira's etailoring skills.

In short order, Cindira located the dress in question, one she had coded just a week or two ago for Kaylie to wear to yet another ball.

There was always *another* ball.

A trail of chiffon and lace danced over the floor as she pulled it from the closet. It was indeed one of her better creations. The secret to its appeal, the tiny twinkling diodes coded into the fabric that made it shimmer in even the dimmest light. Technically, the conception of such a thing would have been flagged by the team in charge of observing and maintaining The Kingdom's esthetic integrity. This was one instance where Kaylie being Kaylie helped Cindira push the boundaries. No one was going to flag something worn by a high-ranking Tybor executive and the step-daughter of Rex Tieg as non-compliant.

Cindira took a moment, studying the gown, conceptualizing its iterations.

"Pele, give me an interface up here."

"Acknowledged."

Like some sort of technical wisp-o-the-willows, a soft glow emerged, a floating tablet filled with numbers, letters, and genius. The code. Most saw only the rudimentary meaning behind the series of symbols, picking out the sections that served to express the augmented representation of each element of the dress floating in the air before her. Cindira saw form, shape, beauty. A few changes, including moving the color from green to yellow and shifting about the pleats and diodes, and the only thing remaining was to follow the template change with the accessories. After which, she hung her creation on the door of the closet, admiring it. It really was quite a gorgeous piece. Elegant, luxurious, yet simple in its form. Kaylie would turn every head in the Palace when she entered wearing it. Cindira reached out, running her fingers over the fabric, imagining the sensation of silk on her palm was real.

"User approaching," Pele announced.

Kaylie must have jacked in early to check on Cindira's work. Which meant it was time to go. Not that her step-sister would see her if she came in. Though Cindira could interact with Kingdom artifacts in the Sink as if she were jacked in, she remained invisible. She instinctually turned to witness the look in her step-sister's eyes when she saw the refashioned dress, the closest thing to appreciation she'd get, when a very unexpected thing happened.

It wasn't Kaylie. It wasn't even Cade or Johanna. Hell, it wasn't even her father, though after two months of the silent treatment, she'd actually welcome that for once.

Who did enter instead was Detective Frank Batista.

"What are you doing here?"

He couldn't hear her. Cindira hadn't engaged the intercom that allowed someone in the Kitchens to be piped into the section of The Kingdom framed in the Sink. If he could have heard her, she'd deliver an inquisition. The Tieg vresidence had been set up with the strictest security protocols. Just because Batista was a member of GAIA's security forces didn't mean he had any special privileges outside of it. With a warrant, he could compel his way in, but there's no way Cindira wouldn't have heard about that. For reasons she didn't understand entirely, she found herself suddenly on the defensive for a family that in turn felt it owed her nothing.

"You should leave," she commanded to dead air, before remembering she had her AI assistant at the ready. "Pele, remove user Frank Batista from this zone. Move him, oh, let's say, fifty feet from the property boundary."

"Cannot comply."

Cindira bit her tongue, reminding herself it was illogical to get angry at something that lacked sentience. "And just *why* can you not comply?"

"No user with that name is in the current zone."

"But I'm looking right at him." Maybe his profile was somehow listed under another name? "Pele, identify the client who is currently in the room with me."

"There are currently no users in this space."

Impossible. "You just told me that a user was approaching. I—"

"User approaching."

Before Cindira could finish talking, the door to the bedroom opened. Vesuvius would admire the way her blood pressure blew up. The form of the condemnation coming her way took shape in her imagination: Kaylie was going to see Batista and point an immediate finger at Cindira's messy security code. There's no way her step-sister would ever believe it had been mere coincidence and being anything but would mean something sinister was afoot.

But as Cindira spun, shouting pointlessly to the detective to leave before he was seen, she discovered the officer had beaten her to the punch.

She was alone.

A smile stretched across Kaylie's face as she saw her remodeled dress hanging on the door of the wardrobe. Cindira's wayward relation walked right through her, oblivious to her presence, her arms held out to embrace the latest creation.

"Perfect!" Kaylie said. "Take that, Maeve. We'll see who Shapur goes home with tonight, won't we?"

As Kaylie began to strip off her Kingdom avatar's default wardrobe, Cindira couldn't get away fast enough.

"Pele, close the window."

In a blink, she found herself looking back at the kitchen through glass much clearer than what she had just seen.

six

The guy did not exist.

Strictly speaking, Cindira knew that wasn't true. Of course, Detective Batista existed. She had seen him, watched him talk with Kaylie, found herself blushing when, for the slightest moment, their gazes had met. He had been real, but the story he'd conjured? Anything but.

Three nights of scrapping through public records after work, and nothing. She needed a break.

She shook the milk carton, relieved to find that there was just enough left for her cup of tea. As much as people liked to joke she was her mother's copy, Cindira differed from Omala on that. Chai must be taken sweet and blond. "Like I like my men," Scotia had once quipped. The hot drink rushed down her throat, a liquid version of meditation that cleared her mind and set her at ease. Cindira crawled under her blanket and pulled the computer on to her lap, determined to find out who in the hell this Batista character really was. More time only brought more frustration.

"How in this age does a person *not* exist online?" Whatever trick he'd used, she wanted to know it. More concerning was why someone would *want* to hide who he really was. The list of motivations that populated in her mind's eye made her shudder.

Maybe if she went to Tybor and scoured the systems directly? Cindira deposited her teacup on the table next to her bed and shuddered again. Okay, so the guy wasn't who he said he was, but that didn't mean he wasn't a potential threat to the company somehow. Creating a trail tied to her employee login investigating his particulars might look like trying to dig up dirt to an outsider. Ironically, it was better to stick to the public places of the web.

She wracked her brain for every bit of information she could remember from her brief observation. Hadn't he said his father had been one of the early representatives to the first GAIA congress? She scoured records, cross-referencing the list of male members with those who also had sons working in the security forces. The few

42

hits she got resulted in profiles that didn't match the interloper's appearance. Just to be fair, she repeated the process with the second and third congresses. Still no match. A fourth search turned up empty as well.

Her fingers hovered over the keyboard, poised but directionless. What else could she do? She'd taken Batista at his word, had no reason to suspect that the man Johanna Tieg referred to as a detective could be anything but.

Johanna. Cindira didn't credit her step-mother with very many positive traits, but one thing she would say of the second Mrs. Tieg was that she ran a tight ship. System integrity and security were paramount items of concern at Tybor, both because The Kingdom's profitability demanded it, but more so because their clientele did. The affluent and the wealthy counted on the platform to be their private playground. Long gone were any innocent notions that participants in the vreal world merely enjoyed the fairytale pageantry, even if that was the way it was marketed. While guidelines and liability considerations led to rules dictating the types of behavior clients could engage in "in public" while jacked in, behind closed virtual doors, anything and everything was game. How, then, had Johanna let an unknown entity into their midst?

Maybe she hadn't. Maybe Johanna was perfectly aware of who Batista really was.

He'd been interested in the architecture behind Tybor's worlds, hadn't he? He'd been young, attractive, open to Kaylie's flirting, even one-upping her to a point that had Cindira herself envious. Batista did everything that was needed to get Kaylie to lower her defenses. Kaylie wasn't Johanna, and she'd let herself be played like an antique synthesizer.

But how did that connect with what she'd witnessed? How had Batista gotten into Kaylie's room? Even if he was Johanna's minion, there was no way Kaylie would have agreed to that intrusion. Not unless they had arranged a clandestine meeting, anyway. Given that the man had mysteriously disappeared the second Kaylie had come into her room, that didn't seem likely.

Cindira threw down her pencil and took to her feet. Maybe the place to look for answers wasn't online, in the great big world, or in a database. Maybe the answers she sought were sitting in the big corner office at Tybor.

She had to know. Not because she cared a lick about what went on in The Kingdom. Frankly, she didn't even really care if the platform disappeared tomorrow. But since it was a clone of GAIA, whatever threatened it, threatened her mother's true legacy as well. Johanna certainly wasn't about to go to bat for it.

Which left Cindira on deck.

She put away her computer, vowing that she'd get her answers when she got to work in the morning.

seuen

Johanna Tieg held the same opinion of rain that she did of her step-daughter; it was a necessary inconvenience that ultimately did a lot of good if she could tolerate its occasional appearance.

Over the edge of her display, Cindira's hands crossed in front of her as she walked into the room. Johanna tapped the button on her headset so she could switch from dictation to manual keying and keep the tail end of the message she was writing private, pausing a moment to hold up one of her long, ringed fingers to request silence. Say what she would about Omala Grover, her predecessor in both the boardroom and the bedroom, at least she had raised Cindira to be compliant. She'd never admit aloud that her own children could have done with a bit more of that in their rearing, but then, she'd rarely admit it to herself either.

Finally, after she'd sent the message requesting an update of tomorrow's plans, she sat back, steepling her hands before her. "Is there something you need, Cindy?"

Cindira assumed a seat across the desk. "Since Kaylie is busy getting a handle of her new position, I thought I could be the one to tell you about the detective's visit to the Kitchens last week."

A lie. They both knew damned well that if Johanna had wanted to know, she would. Assuming she already didn't. Nevertheless, one did have to follow polite social norms until given a reason to do otherwise.

"Oh? Very well, then."

"He wanted to know about the architecture that underlays The Kingdom." Cindira's eyes narrowed almost imperceptibly. "Kaylie told him, as I've told you many times, that most of what makes it function was only known to my mother."

Another lie? Johanna wasn't sure, and it was that uncertainty that kept Cindira both employed and alive.

"Did he believe that?"

The girl's fingers curled around the arm of the chair in which she sat. "It's the truth."

"Of course, it is." Johanna let out a long breath through her nose, pushing herself back from her desk. "But that resurfaces our old, unsolved problem, doesn't it? We *need* to know how it all works. We can't just keep throwing code on top of code. Eventually, we're going to cross some tripwire or make everything too top-heavy, and it's all going to come crashing down."

"Do like I suggested, then. Open up the source code for hacking."

"Hack into it yourself!"

Cindira guffawed. "I'm good, but I'm not that good. I'm not... I'll never be able to do what my mother could."

Not likely. One of the reasons Johanna Tieg had hated Omala Grover so much, was that she never lost appreciation for how talented she was. Even after Johanna had stolen Omala's husband, her company, and her life, she had no doubt that a woman as intelligent as her husband's ex-wife kept files on just how a struggling single mom of two had managed that. *Legally* and *ethically* weren't terms that could be used to describe it. No, there was evidence somewhere in the system. Or at least, there was inside of GAIA, and what was The Kingdom but a GAIA clone monetized and dressed up to look different?

"You mean invite all those underworld tech scum who are constantly launching attacks into our product to do it for pay and with my blessing? I don't think so."

"Fine. Then we'll just figure something out when it does come crashing down." Cindira stood and made to leave, hesitating only a moment later, turning with a finger in the air. "There is one other thing the detective asked."

Johanna's eyes had already picked up where they'd left off on the message she'd been perusing. "Yes, what is it?"

"He asked Kaylie, if she was called in front of the GAIA High Court, would she be able to swear under oath that the source code is unbroachable by anyone."

Johanna's pulse ticked in her forehead. Was Rex's shy and reserved daughter actually baiting her? Fine, if the child wanted to take a turn at the big girl's table, she would give her a sample of the service. "For your sake, you'd better hope so."

But the young woman failed to bend. In fact, Cindira seemed downright unflappable. "Should I talk to my father about this? Is he aware a GAIA security officer was here, snooping around?"

"He's not, and neither you or I will disturb him with that fact. Your father's under a lot of pressure right now. Let him have his space."

Cindira shook her head, her eyes trained to the floor. "I haven't seen or spoken to him for two months now. How much more space should I give him?"

"As much as he needs. He'll let you know when he has time for a visit."

"Good. And please, remind him that I literally live in his backyard. Whenever he has a moment, I'm available."

With that, her step-daughter took her leave.

Johanna pushed back from the desk and tapped her comque, accessing the part of the memory where the image she'd received two months ago was stored. She wasn't sure why she still kept it. She'd looked at it so often, the picture was burned into her mind, along with the message that had accompanied its receipt.

If you ever want to see him again, you know what to do.

But she couldn't bring down GAIA without being able to access the source code, and she couldn't access the source code without also endangering the stability of The Kingdom. She needed to find a way to hack it, in a way that kept as few people involved as possible. The person who undertook the deed could only be someone she could trust not to turn around and use it as leverage against her.

Someone who could stand up to the GAIA Congress, if it came down to it.

Someone like Cindira.

eight

Cindira had been walking for an hour before she'd realized her ventilator's air had soured, but by then, she was already half way across the city, her feet having picked out the path before her head had been clued in.

Even as dusk dissolved and night crept across the east part of town on broken legs and with outstretched hands, she endured. Her father, Johanna, her step-siblings... even most of the people she worked with forgot for whom her mother fought so hard. It was the rich and affluent who strode through marble halls and crystal palaces; it was for the poor and destitute who clung to their crumbling abodes even as the ocean had risen to wash away the old world.

Salt water mixed with city grime, creating a pungent cocktail that threatened to turn her stomach. Cindira walked faster, not from fear, but from determination. How had she allowed fear to become her comfort zone? You couldn't walk with caution towards an awakening, you ran for it full force. Perhaps her agitated state, with her grimace and flexing fists, was the reason no one accosted her. Thinking back on what had happened earlier in the day in Johanna's office further fed her distress.

The biggest difference between a vreal world avatar and an actual person was the tells. The electronic self only mimicked the macro: a hand reaching to pick up a glass, feet stepping in sequence in order to walk, even a sneeze. What it failed to capture and recreate were subtle, unconscious ticks built up over a lifetime: eyes widening when an attractive person came into view, shoulders going back when faced with an obstacle, et cetera. In Johanna's case, a nerve on her temple pulsing when her blood pressure shot up, such as it did when she'd mentioned Batista's question and the possibility of Kaylie testifying.

After the world embraced GAIA's potential, the Ping-Bailenson Act of 2126 consigned all international relations – including wars – of member countries to the meta-authority body. "The hand that turns the screw, while also making all the screws, and the screwdrivers," one journalist of the era had called it. That fact put Tybor, a privately-held company, in an odd position and called for many checks and balances. GAIA might be the one who used the tools which ran the world, but Tybor owned the garage. Under her father's watch, Cindira trusted that the company upheld its promises to not become involved with Gaian politics or policies. Officially, Tybor only supported the VR system without any compensation. A charitable act. A *humanitarian* act. Cindira still believed that to be true, but what if things had gotten to a *quid pro quo* state? If that was the case, she wanted to know what that quid was, and for the that, she was going to have to find the quo.

The last time she'd been in GAIA had been fifteen years before. A lot could change in that amount of time. News reports couldn't be trusted; she knew that much even as a child. She needed to see it with her own eyes. Something told her if she could unravel the mystery surrounding Batista, she'd have a better idea of what was going on.

He answered on the tip of the second buzz. "Go for Mack."

Cindira turned down Market, heading toward the ruins of the San Francisco Ferry Building. "Can you go put in a cameo in the security office and run a little interference?"

"You know most people say hello when they call. It's a basic courtesy."

"So that's a no, then?"

Back at his desk in Tybor, Mackey barked out a laugh on the other end of the comque. "That's like asking me if I can breathe. Of course, I can. But why do you need me? Your clearance is even higher than mine."

She made the final turn, looking four blocks ahead to where the unkempt majesty of ruined skyscrapers dangled their foundations in the surf. A sunken block more, the clocktower still etched on many of the city's tourist kitsch, illuminated under a gibbous moon, kissed its twin image on the calm waves beneath it. "I don't want Tybor records tracing any breach back to a source near the Embarcadero."

Apprehension shaded Mack's voice. "You're in that part of town at this time of night?"

"Don't have much choice. If I jack in from one of Tybor's machines, Johanna will know."

49

"What you up to, Cin? Going to such lengths to get to a seedy jackpod?"

"Seedy has its advantages."

"Yeah, but the Ferries are where all the bootleggers run their knockoffs that feed the chipheads." Cindira pictured Mackey rubbing his right bicep with his left hand. "Where are you? I'm going to tag out and come down there. I don't like you wandering into that part of town alone."

"Absolutely not, I need you in security. Besides, the chipheads revere me. You think they'd ever do anything to hurt the daughter of their Goddess?"

"If you were actually public about that, maybe not. But don't forget, Cin. Everyone reveres their goddess, until she abandons them." His overly-dramatic sigh told her she'd won him over, even if reluctantly. "What do you need?"

"For no one else to notice the unregistered user walking around GAIA."

"GAIA?" His voice pitched up an octave. "What in the Hell are you going in there for?"

"Because I'm the only one who can."

She reached the waterline as the clocks rolled Tuesday into Wednesday. The Ferry Building had once marked the edge of the city, the place where land gave way to sea. About forty years ago, the sea took a share back, reclaiming sidewalks and cafes. Nearest the shore, you could still find pavers that had been laid down in olden times. Forty yards out, the walls of the first story of the landmark building were being eaten away slowly by saltwater, leaving only the steel girders that kept the upper levels aloft. In time, nature would nibble her way through those, too. Officially, the site was condemned. Unofficially, pirate jackers operated from the famous tower, aware that at any moment, an earthquake, tsunami, or plain bad timing could pushout the remaining building beneath them.

Cindira appreciated the reality of it. Foundations toppled all the time; a young girl whose mother died suddenly was all too aware.

"Need passage, love?"

She'd been so fixated on the building, Cindira had neglected to notice the boat bobbing a few feet out, tied to what may have been a lamppost once upon a time. From the darkness, two bloodshot orbs catching ambient light from the city stared out from a face sallow and thin.

"How much to get to the tower?"

"How much you got?"

A spark, then a flicker, and then a flame lit his features.

Cindira's breath caught in her throat at the sight of a mangled twist of sinew and scar tissue, one prominent demarcation that ran from his collarbone, up his neck, and to where the corner of his mouth had healed poorly, leaving the bottom lip longer than the other. On his chin, a tattooed barcode occupied space where once a beard may have grown.

"You're a convict."

"No, love. I'm an ex-con. Survivors have scars." He pulled a long tug from his cigarette and blew out the smoke in a long tunnel. "And heads."

He wore no ventilator mask. The poor rarely had them and paid a debt greater than money for their poverty: shortened lifespans. Cindira stilled herself and silenced the tiny voice in the back of her head telling her only an idiot would get into a skiff with an admitted criminal and head into the night on the very waters where her mother died.

"I can give you sixteen for the trip out."

"The trip out is free. It's the trip back that'll cost you."

"Sixteen for that, then."

"Twenty."

"Eighteen."

"Done."

Pulling an oar from the bottom of the boat, he closed the

distance over the calm water, offering out a hand at the shore. When Cindira reached for him, intending to slide her fingers over his to steady her step down. She almost fell over when he pulled back.

"Money first."

"You said the ride out was free."

"It is, but what if you never come back?"

She ticked up the agreed-upon fee into the bracelet on her wrist, but then paused before putting her finger on the print reader to slide the funds over. "Doesn't everybody?"

"From the tower? You serious?" When she nodded, he continued. "Some don't. Them's the type that likes to get jacked in, but no intention of ever coming back out."

Chipheads. Tybor had its competitors in the VR franchise, of course. Companies that offered an inferior product, like the arena Cindira fought in at The Stadium. Still, the lure of a better – if artificial – life was enough to tempt some people into abandoning reality for good. Not all VR forums had a stroke of midnight protocol like The Kingdom to kick out those who didn't belong.

Cindira pushed the send signal, and the money transfer was done. This time when he offered his aid, she took it readily. Without sea legs, her arms went wide, holding out to the sides and steadying herself as she sat. "But don't they know their bodies atrophy after a while?"

"They go there to die, love. It's a bit of the point. I mean, all them Buddhists talking about Nirvana, isn't that what they're after? Freeing the mind from the body? Makes me wonder if them dead ones ain't still alive somehow, inside those machines." He looked out across the water, wistful in a way that bordered jealousy.

After a few moments, his focus drew back to her. "Pretty thing like you shouldn't waste your life away in some VR opium den or night club. You parlay the right folk, you could get a sugar, get inside The Kingdom even."

The last thing she wanted was some richie who supplied her with jack time in exchange for money and/or lewd acts.

Her chest rose and fell. "I'm going to jack into GAIA."

"The bloody World Order?" The oarsman guffawed. "Tell you what, I'll give you back half your money and take you back now. No point on you going to the Ferries. None of them can get you in there."

"I don't need them to get me in. I just need use of their jackpods and an agreement to look the other direction."

"The other direction's the only way they know how to look in there." He nodded, puffing on his cigarette even as he continued to row. "You'd need to have some serious connections to jack into a system like that. Or be a crack hacker."

She turned back to the edifice towering above. "I do, and I am."

nine

"Don't accept greens."

The surly woman who met her at the door—or the gaping hole in the wall that had once been a window—curled a lip as Cindira's finger hovered over her comque. U.S. Dollars, called "greens" for merely anachronistic purposes, still ruled legitimate markets, but this wasn't exactly Union Square.

"I have crypto." Cindira scrolled through her personal ledgers. "Do you take bot? Or rubbies? I can even pass you kartz, if you're looking for something really exotic."

A chill ran up her spine when the wrinkled woman's claw clutched Cindira's hand. "Lots of variety from someone climbing the tower. Who are you, and why would someone like you come about these parts? You think you're setting me up?"

"I'm here for the same reason anyone else comes here." Cindira loaded two hundred kartz into the transfer tray on her comque, then hit send. The Ferrier's own device buzzed on her wrist, indicating receipt. "Because I'm not really here, if you catch me."

The grizzled woman studied the numbers flashing on her wrist. "That's twice the daily rate."

"And all I need is two hours, a private jackpod, the highest bandwidth you got, and the ability to disable any security protocol you have in place."

"No go. Without my walls, all that dirty water comes slushing in."

"Don't worry, I'm going to build new walls. Everything will stay high and dry."

The Madame's face cycled through resolution, doubt, temptation, and, finally, resignation. "Fine, but I'm going to have my hand over the power button, don't care if the sudden evac scrambles your brain or not."

54

"Fine by me."

"Follow me then."

They walked down a hall with broken tile floors and graffitied walls. Moonlight fell through what must have been an arched glass ceiling at some point. Now, only frame remained, blanketed over by tattered tarps blowing in the wind. Crossing a mezzanine, Cindira's attention hooked onto a familiar set of eyes that pulled her like tractor beams in their direction. The subject of the mural sat in lotus position, her hands open, upturned on her knees. In one hand, a dead earth still smoldered at the edges, and in the other, she held a miniaturized rain forest, verdant and flowing with rivers.

The Madame took turns looking at the mural, then to Cindira. "Anyone ever tell you that you look like her?"

"We're both just Indian is all." Cindira tried to distance any speculation. "Who painted this?"

"Who knows? It's been here longer than I have. The chipheads think she's some kind of patron saint, like her image has the power to keep this building from falling down."

Cindira looked back at the stout woman. "You sound like you don't believe it."

"I don't. Just because she invented GAIA doesn't mean she's divine. This building will fall when the universe decides it should, no matter what we do. Just like this planet will die with or without us, no matter how many Omala Grovers it gives birth to."

For fifteen years, one question had resurfaced in Cindira's thoughts again and again. If she could ever bring herself to do it, if she could ever go back into that place forever tied to the memory of her mother, would it be like they'd left it on that long-ago September day?

At last she had her answer.

The room was the same. Modest, with two twin beds and

a night stand. A closet held a collection of clothing and shoes, the fashions just dated enough to be noticeable. The wallpaper: pale yellow and with white primroses. The mirror in the corner faced the door, but even as Cindira sat up, she saw its angle was just enough to reflect not her own bare feet, but those of the woman lying on the other bed.

Omala's avatar remained right where she'd left it, stretched out on one of two twin beds, as though she may pop into it at any moment. Cindira sat up and waited, half-expecting her mother's eyes to crack open, for her to turn her head her way and say, "Good morning, *pyaari beti*. What new thing shall we learn today?"

The City had been her playground then. The Congress, the Hall of Records, the Archives... even the Palace where the elected Prince held court. Oh, she'd never been permitted to attend court, but she could *imagine* what that had been like. All of her mother's stories helped, of course.

Outside the city, beyond its fortified walls, war raged on in the Arenas, but she'd been too young to understand what that meant, and too innocent to perceive its discussion in conversation. It was incomprehensible now, that this world her mother created, in which the City and its people shone, was merely a pearl trapped in the mire of the oyster's gullet.

The Grover GAIA residence stood apart from the City, while seemingly embedded into its very heart. It was a "magic pumpkin," her mother had called it, a parallel reality built with the same source code and paradigms, but not technically embedded in it. Most of the time, when a person with a vreal world account died, any avatar created for them was permanently archived. Omala's would have been too, if not contained in the safety of this bubble.

Before she knew what she was doing, Cindira was on her knees at her mother's bedside, Omala's hand wrapped in her own.

"Mom." Her heart fluttered in her chest. "Um... Hi. I... I know this isn't really you. I get that. But, well... It's been awhile and... I've said this at your grave too, but just to say it again: You were... You *are* my hero. I look back on the things you've done and the worlds you created and I... They're just so wonderful. You gave the world such a gift, and the only thing you asked for in return was me. It didn't seem like a fair exchange, but I did my best to make it seem like it was. I'm still trying, but Johanna..."

56

She bit back the bitterness, refusing to let that poison seep into this moment.

"I want you to know: I'm still watching out. For Tybor, for GAIA, for The Kingdom. For Dad, when he lets me, but you know how he is."

She imagined her mother laughing, even though the empty avatar remained unchanged.

"Mom, where ever you are, can you watch out for *me*? If you do that, then you're helping to look out for them too. I miss you, and I love you."

She pushed a kiss to Omala's hand, before gently setting it beside her mother's body.

Sunbeams spun of gold and crimson pierced Cindra's eyes as she stepped out of what, looking behind her for a moment, appeared to be a red brick wall. Funny, but she remembered the outside of the 'magic pumpkin' as a wood-framed door with a single pane of stained glass. In fact, she'd seen that door and opened it from the inside just moments before. When she reached for where she thought the doorknob should be, the image waivered. Cindira picked up a piece of stone from a nearby flowerbed and used it to etch a mark. On her return, she'd be certain to know the way out. She could exit the program from anywhere, but if GAIA still had the same security protocols as it'd had when she was younger – as the copied world of The Kingdom still had – the AI embedded into the source code would scan the environment each night at midnight. Any unregistered entity would be wiped clean. If she left her avatar behind, even hidden, she'd never be able to return to it again.

The avenue led to the main square, beyond which another promenade would carry her to Congressional Hall. Few souls roamed the streets this early in the day. The Gaian time zone aligned with the city that had inspired the design of this part of the vreal world, The Hague, as it had existed about two hundred or so years before, also meaning it was hours ahead of the local time in San Francisco. Cindira had always admired this choice made by her mother, not only to design a vreal world so intense in its reality as to deceive the human mind, but styled after a period of history in which rich fabric, marbled motifs, and gold-gilded mosaics were all the rage. Every design rang true, from the grand clock tower ticking out the minutes on the Palace gate, to the intricately-fitted tiles on the floors within it.

She'd never been taken outside the safety zone of the City, so she couldn't know if the war arena had changed or not. From the nightly shows, where captures of national 'battles' taking place within GAIA doubled as entertainment, she knew that they'd endured, however. Cindira shuddered to think what life was like before her mother's creation, when you lived under the threat of war, anything could hide a bomb, and anyone could be a terrorist. She'd often wondered if living through the fall of London was what had inspired her mother's concept of GAIA in the first place.

Just imagine it: a city that could never fall, and war that could never destroy.

Enough reminiscing, Cindira thought. *To work.*

While his name may have been made up, Cindira suspected Batista's claim to have been part of GAIA's Security Force wasn't. After seeing him in Kaylie's room, she assumed he specialized in cybersecurity. It would take one hell of a crack hacker to infiltrate Alsace, and that kind of talent didn't work blue. Was he a criminal, and his whole charade full of evil intentions? Still a possibility, but she'd investigate this part of it first.

The Hall of Records occupied a long road of townhouses, three stories high and running on for two blocks near the Palace. If she could get inside, Cindira could wire into their records and search through profile photos for one that looked like Batista. She was a few steps from the stoop leading to the entry when a hand wrapped around her arm and delicately pulled her back.

She wouldn't have to look for Batista's picture. The man stood right before her. Curious, he was dressed the same way he'd been in real life, down to the antiquated watch on his wrist.

He blinked twice, three times. When he spoke, it was both with amusement, and an undertone of rebuke. "Children aren't allowed into this building."

"What children?" *But I'm not a...*

But she was. At least, her avatar was, and unless the rules had changed, that meant, from Frank Batista's perspective, she *must* be a child. Gaian protocol didn't allow for minor avatars except in the case of actual children. It didn't matter. In fact, it couldn't hurt that she appeared to be her younger self. If Batista recognized her from Tybor, who knew what trouble that could cause. Tensions between

58

GAIA and her father's company were tense enough. If he thought she were here as a spy...

But she was, wasn't she? Only, not for Tybor. And it's not like he wasn't at Tybor snooping around either.

"Are you lost?"

Cindira snapped back to the moment. "Not exactly."

He let go of her arm when he seemed certain she wouldn't bolt and looked around. "You here with a school group or a parent? You know you're not supposed to wander around on your own. Even if it is a virtual environment, security is very tight. Someone might think you were up to something."

"I..." What could she say? "I'm here with my mom, but she's... I lost her."

In the worst of ways.

"Okay, then..." His face broke into a smile, and she felt something melt deep within her. "Let's get you unlost and back to your mother. What's your name?"

"Cin... Cindy," she lied, the quiver of guilt within turning electric when she realized the opportunity it had presented her. "What's yours?"

His head tilted. "Been a while since anyone here had to ask. Feels a little funny. You sure you don't know?"

He'd said it with such lightness, she wasn't sure if he was being coy or arrogant.

"No, I'm sorry. Should I?"

"So the secrecy protocols are working," he said, seemingly more to himself then her. "That should make Carlos happy. You can call me Francisco."

Francisco, not Frank. She made a mental note to rerun her searches using the amended knowledge. For the moment, she had to be careful not to blow her cover. "That's the same name as the prince, isn't it?"

"It is." Francisco's mouth dropped open in mock surprise.

When he wasn't acting like an indifferent authoritarian, he was quite charming. "It's a very common name, though. But I'll let you in on a little secret. He's not as handsome as I am."

No doubt of that. No one knew what the real Prince Francisco looked like. His real-world identity was a state secret, a way of protecting his physical body from harm while he was jacked into GAIA. Cindira was willing to bet, however, that some stuffy old politician couldn't claim such deep brown eyes or have the defined, perfected cheek bones that this Francisco had. Whoever had sculpted his avatar should be given a major award.

Reminding herself that she'd seen Francisco in the real world, however, she realized that the artist responsible for this work was one of divine origins.

Or, at least, *really* good genetics.

"Now, where should you be?" He surveyed the street. "Don't suppose you know which direction you came from?"

"I was with my class. We're touring the City." She bit her tongue too late. Lying wasn't an art in which she was well-practiced, but she had better get good, and fast. One of Francisco's eyebrows took on a precarious angle. Already his reaction was telling her she'd messed up somehow. "The last place I recognized was Ferreira Square."

"I thought you said your mom brought you here?"

"She did. She's one of the chaperones."

"Right..." With balled fists on hips, Francisco stared at a patch of ground. "Ferreira Square? You sure about that?"

"Pretty sure. It's where they swore in the first congress, right? I recognized it from my... lesson docs?"

"Is that so?"

An invisible hand reached into her stomach and squeezed. She'd said something wrong, but what? "I could be wrong. Maybe I—*ahh!*"

The experience of pain inside of GAIA? That was new. It was not, however, welcome. As Francisco gripped Cindira by the wrist, squeezing away her confidence, storm clouds gathered in his eyes.

"What's the name of your school?"

"My..." *Whimper.* "Musk Preparatory!"

Not her actual high school, but the one her mother had wanted her to go to before she died. Johanna had had other plans, ones that took her far away from San Francisco and her father. Still, she shouldn't have said it.

"There is no group here today from Musk Preparatory!" His teeth clenched, and with it, his grip. "And you couldn't have been in Ferreira Square. Your people destroyed it two weeks ago!"

"Destroyed it?" She fell to her knees, gasping. "*My* people?"

With a twist, her hands flattened to the street. Francisco pulled his comque to his mouth. "Security, triangulate my location and identify the user nearest me. Seems one of the hackers has crawled out of the shadows."

"I'm not a hacker!" A lie. And her pride in those very abilities made its taste the most bitter on her tongue. "I'm here with my school group. I—"

"There are no school groups here today from anywhere. Now, maybe if you tell me who you really are and what your people are trying to accomplish by destroying GAIA piece by piece, we can—"

Cindira was too stunned to respond. *Someone's destroying my mother's work? But how? The City is safe, the code is unbreakable—*

"Warning: explosion imminent. Vacate area."

The matter-of-fact tone of the system notification brought them both to a standstill. Francisco, because of the implication, she reckoned. Cindira, because the voice was her mother's.

Francisco pulled Cindira's arm, jerking her away. "Hurry, run! Get out of—"

Wait. He was *helping* her now? Just after accusing her of being an anarchist, he was trying to save her?

She'd have listened to him, if it had been within her power. But she couldn't run. She couldn't move. Cindira couldn't do... anything.

Intense, utter pain wracked her body from the inside out.

Before her, Francisco called out for the briefest of moments. And then he was gone.

Only when Cindira hit her head against the glass of the jackpod and felt the real-world sweat dripping from her forehead did she realize she was out. Not by choice, but by force. And she could never go back to GAIA again.

There'd be nothing to go back to. Her avatar died in the explosion.

ten

Scotia MacAvoy grabbed the bat she kept next to her bed. The Inner Mission wasn't a hotbed of criminal activity, but common sense dictated certain precautions. Her pulse slowed as she realized the person pounding on her door at 3 AM wasn't trying to get in by force, but by desperation. Nonetheless, she remained vigilant as she tiptoed to the door and flicked on the preview screen. A hologram a mere few inches tall displayed at eye level, represented the woman on the other side.

"Cindira?" Scotia flung the door open, catching her breathless friend as she collapsed into her arms. "Oh, my god, what happened?"

Cindira struggled to get the words out. "I ran... here... once I got to... shore."

"Shore? What do you mean shore? Were you out on the bay?"

Cindira recovered her feet and drove forward. But not for the couch, as Scotia had supposed, but for the TV. The wall flickered to life as Cindira scrolled through the stations, past late-night advertisements and reruns of the ancient programs people called flat flickers.

"No, the Ferries." Wide-eyed, Cindira turned on her. "Local channels?"

Scotia closed the door and called on her in-home artificial intelligence assistant. "Tyra, tune to channel six, please."

Tyra quickly obeyed her master, even though her master had no idea why the hell she was asking.

Cindira's breathing normalized as she and Scotia took a seat on the couch. On the wall, the local channel appeared to be showing a rerun of a daytime soap, only with the mostly Caucasian and Latino actors modulated to Chinese.

"Impossible."

"Oh, wait, that's my fault. I was practicing my Mandarin earlier. Tyra, please switch the spoken language to American."

"I don't mean the language." Cindira was on her feet again, pacing. "Tyra, bring up a preview screen of all news channels, local, national, and international."

Two beeps proceeded Tyra's serene twill. "Guest access authorized?"

Scotia acknowledged it. The wall segmented into dozens of tiny boxes, each displaying a thumbnail version of the channel it represented. Cindira pecked at the wall, wiping away options with her gestures, growing more restless when each image increasing in size proved to be as unsatisfactory as the last.

"No, no! It's not possible! Someone has to know. *Someone has to be covering it!*"

Scotia studied her friend's reaction, reading the confusion through a furrowed brow that soon turned into a huff of frustration.

"Tyra, TV off. Cindira—" Scotia pivoted. "—it's three-thirty in the morning. What's this about?"

Her friend ran a hand through her silken black hair. "There was an explosion. Inside GAIA. Thirty... No! *Forty* minutes ago."

"There are always explosions in GAIA. It's a war zone."

Cindira shook her head. "Not in the city. I was just there, I was—"

"Wait, you were *in* GAIA?" Confusion wasn't quite the right term for what Scotia was feeling. Bewilderment? That might do.

"Yes! I saw it. I was there. I..." She swallowed, all color draining from her olive complexion. "I was where it happened. I... blew up."

"Don't be ridiculous. It couldn't have..." But the look in her friend's face told her she wasn't lying. Or at least, as far as Cindira was concerned, she was speaking God's honest truth. But that didn't make any sense. "You'd need an exceptionally high security clearance to be able to get into GAIA without some sort of official invite or sponsorship."

"I hacked in."

64

"Oh, well then." What other holes could Scotia poke in this to get her friend to come back to reality? "But even then, you'd need an avatar, and you don't have one."

"I said I don't *currently* have one. I did have one before my mother died."

"So, let me get this straight…" Scotia pushed the thumb and index finger of her left hand into her temple. "You've had an avatar inside of GAIA, hidden somewhere and no one found it? Where?"

"Inside a magic pumpkin." When Scotia stared at her, slack-jawed, Cindira continued. "That's what my mom always called them anyway. Rooms that run parallel to the vreal world but aren't technically part of it."

"Right." Scotia pushed an index finger into her chin. "And to stay off grid, last night you went to the Ferries to hang out with a bunch of chipheads and hack your way into GAIA."

"Not technically into GAIA. I'm not sure if even *I'm* capable of that. I went into the magic pumpkin. It, in turn, bridged to GAIA."

"And inside GAIA, the very guy you were looking for just… happened to find you. And then everything exploded."

"I know it sounds crazy but…"

Cindira's voice trailed off as her eyes went unfocused. Scotia knew that look, the one that said her friend wasn't thinking in words at the moment, but in code. After a few moments, she snapped her fingers in time with the lightning striking her brain. "That must be it! It *didn't* happen. What I perceived as an explosion was just a security measure. The system recognized my avatar as an unregistered entity and blasted me out. Yes. Yes, that must be it. It couldn't have been a *real* explosion, right? How would that even happen in the city?"

Scotia pulled at the threads she could grasp. "GAIA is a platform designed, in part, for mankind to fight its wars in an environment where no one would be actually hurt. You want to know how an explosion happened *there*?" She pushed a hand against her friend's brow. "What did you take? Did someone sneak you something?"

"I'm fine." Cindira's frigid fingers pulled Scotia's hand from her brow. "I must sound like one of the chipheads in your studies."

"Not really, you're not paranoid enough." Scotia shrugged. "I don't think anyone becomes a chiphead in just one night. Just tell me what happened, as best as you remember it."

"Remember that guy that was at the announcement of Kaylie's promotion? The one you thought might be on the Board?"

"Yeah, the cute one."

Cindira nodded. Good to know she wasn't the only one who thought so. "I was at Tybor, fixing up Kaylie's dress inside The Kingdom—"

"What?" Scotia held up a hand as she pushed her way into the conversation. "I thought we agreed you were going to tell her to go to hell if she did that again. Cindira, you've got to learn to stand up for yourself. Stop letting the Terrible Two push you around."

"That's not the point. Just listen, please?" Her begging proved pitiful enough to win sympathy. And silence. "I was in Kaylie's room in The Kingdom, in the simulator, and *he* showed up there."

Scotia's hands went to her gaping mouth. "Did he see you?"

"No, he was like a… like a… ghost, or something."

"There's no such thing as ghosts. Not in the vreal world, not in this one. Besides, you put up the security parameters around Alsace yourself. There's no way someone could have gotten in without you having validated their profile."

"You mean, the way no one could get inside GAIA without the right credentials?" The brunette laughed under her breath at her own rebuke. "There aren't many as good at hacking Tybor systems as I am, but there has to be a few people out there. But if Frank… *Francisco*, it actually turns out, were such a crack hacker, why would he risk exposing his identity by coming to Tybor, anyway?"

A diode in Scotia's memory illuminated. She grabbed her comque from its charger on the side table. "I may be terrible with faces, but I'm great with names. Do you know his last name?"

"Johanna introduced him to Kaylie as Frank Batista, but that was probably a lie too."

Batista. Of course. Scotia smiled. "One might argue that anglicizing a name isn't really lying about it; it's just reinterpreting it.

Adapting to an American standard rather than a Spanish one is more redaction than dishonesty."

"You're saying he was lying..." Cindira's head cocked to the side. "...by telling a *version* of the truth?"

Her red hair bounced on her shoulders as she nodded. "It's something *politicians* are famous for. Ah, here we go."

Only a few weeks before, Scotia had been asked to present a report inside of GAIA on her research, at a session attended by several high-ranking politicians. In general, and for security, the representations of avatars of such elite were kept secret. Still, Scotia managed to get permission to click off one picture, with the caveat that it was for private use only.

"He wasn't introduced, but he came into the hearing room half way through my presentation, and you could just tell he was important by the way everyone got all awkward in their seats. Afterward one of the congressmen told me who he was. I don't think anyone realized I got him in my picture, or they probably wouldn't have let me keep it." She double-tapped her comque, making the tiny image on the flexible screen on her wrist pop out as a proportional holographic display. "That's him, isn't it?'

Her friend's bloodshot eyes nearly popped out their sockets. Cindira lunged forward, grabbing Scotia's wrist and angling the tiny projected image to a better vantage point. "It is! Who is he?"

Most people who worked with Cindira Tieg considered her a genius. But as with most geniuses, a surplus of savvy had been paid through a debit against other areas of knowledge. In her case: current events. Scotia didn't consider it a fault. It was what it was. Cindira could ramble off from memory Pi to sixty places or recite on demand the latest policies adopted by the International Commission on Alt-Reality Standards, but ask who the current mayor of San Francisco was or which two actors were rumored to be dating, and she threw you anime eyes.

All that was left was for Scotia to state the obvious. "Cindira, you were talking to Francisco Batista de la Reina, the Prince of GAIA."

Denial took control of Cindira's body, making her hands shake. "Impossible. Why would the prince make his avatar look exactly like he really looks?"

"Why indeed? Not that *I'm* complaining." Scotia bit her lip as she again double tapped the device on her wrist. The image disappeared, as did Scotia's patience with middle-of-the-night intrigues. "Questions, I'm afraid, that will wait for a more respectable time of the morning. We both need to get some rest. Stay here, at least until sunrise. We'll start figuring it out together. If you need something to help you sleep..."

"I don't."

Scotia set her comque back on the charger. "Good. You know, it's too bad I didn't know about that avatar you had. I might have wanted to borrow it. Hardly anyone gets to go into the high security zone. Why haven't you visited GAIA all these years?"

"Because I don't belong there, Scotia. I'm just a code writer. I'm not a diplomat, and I'm certainly not a warrior."

Scotia smiled. "Yeah, tell that to Barrel."

eleven

Try as she may, sleep refused to come. Cindira lay on Scotia's pull-out sofa, her hands laced over her stomach, her eyes making patterns of the random blots splotched all over the textured ceiling. Questions were demanding hobgoblins, ones which seem to double with every answer she suggested.

Why had Batista shown up at Tybor alone, claiming to be nothing more than a detective? Why not just send an actual GAIA security agent? Was the prince in the habit of traipsing about the real world without guards? Maybe he couldn't trust his own security detail? But if he wasn't communicating with them, who had helped him get into such a secure part of The Kingdom? Why was he so interested in the source code?

Why had getting booted from GAIA felt like an explosion?

Cindira wished she could shut down her mind the way she could shut down one of her computers. As she heard the sound on the floor beside her, however, she was glad to be awake. If not, the shock of something scurrying across the room and leaping up on the end of the mattress might have set her off screaming. Instead, she moved with the stealth of a ninja, slowly extending her arm to the side table where the cup of water Scotia had given her before going back to bed sat empty. Fingers curled around the plastic vessel. Rat or mouse or squirrel even, she'd probably miss hitting it, but hopefully she could scare it away.

The creature began to scuttle, zipping left, then right, inching up the bed. Cindira gave herself a moment of pep talk, drew down a lungful of courage, and sprang up as she simultaneously heaved the tumbler.

Lamps flickered on overhead as the sensors along the walls tripped. The light brought no meaning, and only further illuminated her confusion.

The mouse stared at the intended weapon where it had landed on the mattress next to him. Turning to Cindira, his tiny black eyes blinked twice before he opened his mouth and did the impossible.

"Well, *that* was uncalled for!"

Cindira scrambled back against the couch cushions. "I'm going crazy." Hallucinations were common among the chipheads. She didn't jack in *that* much, did she? She pushed fingers into her forehead. "Maybe I have a tumor? Oh my god, I have a tumor."

"Madame, you do *not* have a tumor. In fact, I was able to complete a full diagnostic of all your vital systems when you logged into your avatar last night and can confirm that, other than typical aging, your health has experienced no significant changes in the last fifteen years. By the way, it was about time you showed up. I was beginning to think you were never jacking in again."

"You ran a diagnostic? When I was in..." *GAIA.* Which she hacked into illegally. Well, technically, entered without direct authorization, which was basically the same thing. "I don't know what you're talking about. More than that, I don't know *how* you're talking. Mice. Don't. Talk."

"That's true." The mouse blinked twice, wiggled its little nose, and took a few steps forward. "But then again, I'm not really a mouse, as you'll recall. It's me, Laporte."

"My issue isn't remembering your name. The issue is that you are *talking* and I am *crazy.*"

The mouse fell into deep completion. Which, of course, a rodent could probably manage if he could also talk. "You must have blocked me out, associated me with your mother around the time of her death. I'm not sure how to proceed now. The possibility that you would have no recollection of me is not one for which I made any contingencies. Human memory is such a horrendous design flaw. In light of that, the best option, in my opinion, would be to enact the parameter of the least likely scenario, for which I did prepare."

Despite the idiocy of engaging in conversation with a figment of her imagination, curiosity got the better of Cindira. "What was the least likely scenario you thought of?"

"That you would attempt to smash me with a large, heavy object. With your permission, may I run that scenario?"

Why did she nod?

70

"Very good. Madame, I beg you, put down the *name of heavy object* and listen. I've come to warn you, you are in great danger."

twelve

Muscles tight, pulse racing, nails digging into the heel of his hand, drawing blood.

Medics descended as soon as his consciousness shifted realities, but that moment—the one the blaze blew away his skin and shredded his body—held eternity on the balance of a crescent.

Francisco seethed as the real-world reclaimed him. He had *not* been in an explosion. He had not been blown into a dozen pieces. He had *not* just watched an intruder masquerading as a child be killed. *Dios*, he prayed it hadn't been an actual child. It was mere vreal world illusion. His avatar had been sacrificed at the altar of peace, not his mortal form. Avatars were replicable, rewritable.

But wired into the system, his mind still processed the pain as though it had happened, and it hurt like a son of a bitch.

Flailing arms and a wracked body surrendered as his guards pinned him down, keeping him from hurting himself and any others trying to attend him. Carlos's voice gave him a beacon on which to grasp.

"You're back, Your Highness. It wasn't real. This is real. This is the world."

He clung to the truth as his lifesaver, conquering his panicked mind. "Explosion," he gasped out. "Another explosion." His hand went to his father's old watch on his wrist, as if the destruction of it in avatar form had somehow destroyed the real one as well.

"Yes, sir," Carlos confirmed. "How many times have I told you, you're going to work yourself to death, coming in so early and staying so late."

The attempt at humor fell flat as Francisco's heart rate began to stabilize. The building could be recoded. Not that it would need to be. Blessed Omala's world was so well fashioned, all the original structures healed themselves. Eventually. *Usually*. Avatars, required to be recoded from scratch, took actual human labor to reconstruct, though Francisco found the process faster by not requiring his

72

people to make too many modifications. An hour or so in a whole-body scanner, a few more by his designers, and the prince would be reborn. As often as he was coming under attack these days, it was the only practical solution—even if it did mean it consequently exposed his real-world likeness.

As the tension began to ease and Francisco regained his senses, his thoughts turned to the consequences. He pushed the security guards and doctor gently away, assuring them that he was okay.

"Damage?"

"A few buildings in the immediate vicinity, and the street, of course. The architects estimate Congressional Hall will fully restore itself in twelve days."

He doubted it. Whatever strips of code the rebels had used to blow up Ferreira Square left the area unrepairable. The explosion had destroyed it down to the source code, a play that Tybor itself admitted it couldn't touch. Francisco expected the Congressional office buildings would prove to have sustained the same kind of damage.

Someone was trying to destroy GAIA piece by piece. Only this time, the fact that they'd sent in an agent to intercept him in the target area suggested their goals might not end with the platform; they might extend to the Congress itself.

Carlos slid shoes on to Francisco's feet. "We've called off sessions for the day and alerted both Congress and their staff, as a precaution."

"Damn it, Carlos, tell me about the girl!" He sat up, shaking the sweat from his hair. "Do we know who she was yet?"

Carlos's dark brow fretted. "The girl, sir?"

"The one whose arm I was holding when the explosion hit. We need to find out how she wandered so far into the secure zone alone. Get out across the wires, too, and make sure no one hears about this latest attack."

Maybe that was what that girl's role had been: a witness. After GAIA officials had been able to squash the news of the previous three attacks in the city from leaking, the rebels must be growing frustrated, not getting the righteous outrage they had expected. If there was a witness, however, one who likely had been backing up her POV on some external source so she could run to the media with it later, that cat would soon be out of the bag. Unless they found her first.

When Carlos stayed mum, Francisco's anger finally broke. "Come on, people, it's a basic username query. I know you don't know code, but you can handle a whois request, can't you?"

"Sir, it's not that. It's just..." The valet swallowed his nerves. "As I already said, you were the only user in the vicinity at the time. There wasn't a child. There wasn't anyone else."

"But that's impossible. She was..."

A dark truth hit the prince's mind all at once. "She was the bomb, Carlos."

"Sir?"

Francisco slid off the bed and hurried to one of the system panels in the control room of the GAIA jackpod. A few taps in the historical ledger brought up the stories he remembered reading a few weeks ago in the dossier prepared for him. Since GAIA's launch, so few real-world skirmishes occurred, the practice of many of the ways of resistance and war had been forgotten in the previous generation. At last, he found the file and pulled it up.

"A suicide bomber," Francisco declared, enlarging the article so his deputy could see. "Innocence, Carlos. It's probably the one trap that works on me."

"But sir," the deputy continued, "even if she was a suicide bomber, *she* would still show up in the records. There were no other avatars in the region of the explosion."

Francisco gnashed his teeth. He knew what he knew, no matter what the system reported. "I'm almost starting to think your advice to activate my bodycam inside the platform wasn't so crazy."

Hope lit Carlo's eyes. "I'll do so immediately, sire."

"No!" Francisco held up a hand. "I said *almost*. I'm just going to have to figure out some other way to document these things, but I still don't understand why the system didn't detect that user."

Had it been a glitch? Had the child not really been there? She couldn't have been a VAPOR, could she? As far as he knew, Virtual Automated Persons, Objects, and Relics only existed in the later iteration of Omala's world structure, not in GAIA. In The Kingdom, the programs which resembled animate beings, be it a person, a dog, or a fairy, were used to flesh out the experience, so to speak. But humans who were programs were marked between the eyes, a mirrored bhindi revealing them as what they really were. The child had no such marker.

And that fact left only one other possibility.

Francisco grabbed a bottled water from the fridge under his desk and took a swig. "A ghost in the machine."

"Sir?"

The prince turned. "Omala Grover wrote about it in some of her early theoretical work, the ones in her university files that were never published. She theorized that if a person were to die in the real world while they were logged in to a robust platform, the neural emulator would effectively allow their avatar to carry on without any knowledge that the body and soul it was based on had passed. There would no longer be a connection from outside the program; our current interfaces wouldn't see the user as being in the space because, technically, they wouldn't be, just their avatar would."

Every additional word made Carlos's features twist a little more. "But what you're saying then, is that this girl who approached you…"

"Was already dead," the prince completed the conclusion for him. "She was a suicide bomber, but she'd probably actually died hours before. Maybe her avatar's presence was meant to trigger the bomb when she made sure I was actually in the area. But that doesn't mean someone couldn't have found a way to lift her POV data and store it somewhere. Damn it, come to think of it, she might have been an innocent all along. She sure did seem surprised when I turned on her."

And when the building exploded, he *had* seen the panic in her eyes.

He dropped the empty bottle into the recycling bin and wiped his mouth with his sleeve. "We'll figure that part out later. For now, just make sure the story doesn't get out. If I find out Johanna Tiegs knows how far the rebels have been able to damage us, before I tell her myself, I'm going to be pissed."

thirteen

"Asla, you here?"

The house kept its silence. Cindira hadn't expected the old nanny to be home at this time of day; she'd be in the main house, working until five or six. Despite the fact that Cindira begged her to stop, that she didn't need to, that she'd beg Johanna to hire a different housekeeper. But if there was one thing Asla refused to do, it was to put Cindira into a position where she'd need to ask "the old harpy" for anything, even asking her to employ Asla as a favor to her.

"The coast is clear. Come on."

Cindira reached into her coat pocket and opened her hand. Laporte's tiny feet tickled her palm. The tug of his little claws surprised her. For something that wasn't even real, how could he still be so authentic?

She took a seat at the kitchen bar as she set Laporte on the countertop. Just like a real mouse, he set about his grooming with hasty urgency in between polite conversation.

"Thank you, Madame, though we must find another way for me to travel with you. Not that your coat pocket is unpleasant, only I do not like being unable to see."

"Sorry, but I wasn't prepared to be an animal carrier." She grabbed an apple from a bowl of fruit and took a bite, continuing to talk around a full mouth. "Tell me again why you don't want Asla to see you. She must remember you."

"We don't know who we can or can't trust yet." As much as a robotic mouse could, Laporte looked apologetic. "For now, my continued existence must remain need-to-know."

"Just out of curiosity, does that include anyone else besides me?"

"No." He blinked twice. "And I've only come to you now because your recent actions made it necessary. I am doing you no favors to be near you. If my presence is discovered, I fear the repercussions."

The context of that comment did not elude her. No doubt Johanna would love to get her hands on something with so much direct knowledge of Omala's work. "Just how long have you been monitoring me?"

"From a distance, since your mother died. But when you started working at Tybor, I came back to the city. Luckily, nothing you did put you in harm's way. Until last night."

So much had happened all at once, Cindira at first didn't remember the major life moment less than twelve hours ago. "I don't understand why visiting GAIA would be such a big deal. I've been there before."

"Not since The Kingdom launched. The fact that an explosion occurred precisely where you were during the brief time you were there? I don't believe it's coincidence."

"Are you saying I was the target?" She nearly choked as she gulped down an oversized chunk of fruit. "One, why would someone be trying to blow up my avatar? And two, I didn't know I was going until about 10 PM last night. I don't see how they'd know to expect me."

As much as a mouse could grimace, Laporte did. "That is a query for which I haven't found a reasonable explanation."

"Someone had a bot looking for my neural network signature." Her analytical brain shot into gear. "The question is...who, and for how long?"

"That's two questions, actually." The mouse managed to shake his head. "It is also possible that the attack was indeed meant for the prince, and your presence mere coincidence. After all, the other two explosions clearly had nothing to do with you."

"Two *other* explosions?" Cindira shot to her feet. When she'd learned there'd been one before her arrival, that was frightening enough. "So GAIA has covered up two attacks? How?" Cindira ran her hands through her thick, black hair. "And how do *you* know any of this?"

"Because I'm Laporte."

His answer was so simple, it took her a moment to realize she had actually heard him correctly. "Right."

"Madame, I'm a botic. The purpose behind my design makes the answer obvious."

"Hardly. I've seen botics. They're simple devices for people who want a pet without having to feed or clean up after it. Besides, I'm still not entirely sure I haven't gone insane and am imagining you right now. This could all be a dream, my mind creating ways to rationalize the trauma of having been blasted into pieces last night." Cindira remembered the mouse she'd seen in the arena as she'd fought Barrel. And again, the one that crossed her path outside her own gate. Was her brain taking the coincidence and creating this fantasy as a form of self-protection? Or was there something else going on?

"Do you believe that's what's happening?" He waited patiently for her answer.

"I have a near-perfect memory. I'm famous for it, actually. I've remembered things that never happened before, but I've rarely forgotten something that had."

Laporte continued. "Even if you did remember, it may not help. You thought I was a toy, no matter how many times your mother would firmly remind you I was anything but."

"In my defense, I considered most objects toys. The whole world was my playground, and what I couldn't find, I made up. I used to tell everyone that I had too many dreams to waste time awake."

The past kindled in her memory, a mostly happy childhood in which she'd been precocious and curious and brave and inquisitive, and her mother had encouraged her every impulse to learn, to dream, to explore.

As long as she was in bed on time each night.

"Why did she make you look like that, by the way?" Cindira asked, pushing back memories as she tossed the apple core into the garbage. "I mean, you are an impressive piece of tech. I don't think I've seen a botic anywhere near as realistic as you. Definitely not as small. Why make you look like a dirty street rodent?"

"Affronts to my personal sense of self-worth aside, it was a protective measure." The mouse hedged his answer. "No one would look at me and think I was a device capable of monitoring GAIA anytime, day or night. That I could be omnipresent inside of the world, your mother's portal into her creation. I can tap all its records, search logs, review—"

Cindira jumped up. "You can access the source code!" She covered her own mouth when she realized what she'd said, as though someone might be listening. "If Johanna knew, she'd be after you in the blink of her surgically-sculptured eyes."

"Exactly, Madame," the mouse concurred in his balanced accent, slicing together Americana and British. "There are others who would also relish an opportunity to hack your mother's work. No one's VR programs have ever been so well designed. Just look at what Tybor was able to do making a copy of GAIA, and that was only using it as a base and building atop of it. It made your mother furious to find out what Rex and Johanna had done behind her back."

Weakened with the weight of a truth she had suspected all her life, Cindira sank into a nearby chair. "So my father lied; The Kingdom *wasn't* my mother's idea."

"No, and if she hadn't died that night, I'm certain she would have found a way to destroy it."

The echo of memories reverberated in Cindira's head. She didn't remember Laporte, or did she? She had always had a vague memory of someone accompanying her mother to the party on Angel Island the night she died, but those who were there reported Omala had been alone.

"Were you with her when it happened?"

"I was wondering when that would come up." The mouse's head dipped. "It is with deepest regrets that I must tell you I do not know what happened. At the time your mother fell into the water, I was running some rather complex tasks that temporarily shut down my animatronic functions. When I woke up, so to speak, I was floating in the Bay and low on battery. I was able to make it to shore after a few days of swirling around in the tides, but by then your mother was no more. I am sorry, by the way. For your loss, I mean. I know it's been many years, but I do not doubt the pain remains."

The pain of losing the most important person in the world to you at the age of eleven? Of being ripped from your childhood home and sent to boarding school thousands of miles away within months? Of your father abandoning his place in your life to raise another woman's children with tenderness and affection while barely giving you the time of day? Of being forced to devote your working life to supporting a program you'd just learned exploited your mother's work without her consent?

Yes, the pain lingered.

"Thank you, Laporte." She inhaled through her nose, centering her thoughts. "You said I was in great danger. What did you mean?"

"You have the same liability that I have. You can access the source code that underlies GAIA and The Kingdom."

She choked on the accusation. "You know that's not true."

It is true, a voice deep within her said.

An even deeper voice shot back, *I know the language of the source code, that doesn't mean I can access it!*

Laporte's little white head tipped to the side. "Perhaps you've forgotten that as well. Perhaps, like your memories of me, it's there somewhere, buried, like having the map to a secret treasure, but no ship or shovels to unearth it."

She wasn't sure what kind of reaction he was waiting for, so she said nothing. After a few moments, however, the little mouse roused himself from his reverie and changed the subject.

"Did you not receive the package I sent?"

Her nose wrinkled. "What package?"

"The one with the shoes. I had it sent here several days ago."

The shoes? "Those were from you?"

Cindira jumped up and rounded the corner of the kitchen. The box still lay on the counter where a few days previously, Kaylie had eyeballed and ridiculed the contents with the most dismissive tone she could muster. Cindira snatched the items from the box and sped back to the mouse.

"They're here, though I'm not really sure what I'm supposed

to do with a pair of glass shoes."

"They are not merely shoes. They're mobile jacks."

Kaylie had mentioned the same thing, but that didn't make it any more a reality. "There's no such thing."

"There are no others, that is for certain," Laporte concurred. "One researcher in India came close to developing something, but he made a fatal flaw in the design. He thought the shoes should be jackpod and processor, in addition to VR renderers."

That was it, the fantasy died. "I hate to tell you this, but those are the three essential elements of achieving a VR presence, so he was kinda right."

"Oh, that *is* completely correct. But, they need not be all in the device itself. In fact, outsourcing the processor is what makes the technology possible."

"But even with that being true – and I don't see how that would work unless the processor was in constant, close proximity – it doesn't solve the problem of energy. The amount of power needed would—"

"Be derived from a combination of solar and kinetic energy harvesting," Laporte again interrupted. "I know you think we're having a theoretical conversation right now, Madame, but you don't seem to understand that the device you're holding was how your mother accessed the worlds she created. You're right about one thing, though. The processor could not be small enough to fit into a shoe."

"Where is it then?"

The mouse blinked twice. "I'm looking at her."

Fourteen

In the second time in as many weeks, Francisco Batista de le Reina, Elected Prince of GAIA, walked into the corner office of the woman who held him and world peace hostage in every way but physically.

"Hello, Johanna." The blond snake removed her glasses and looked up from her desk, grinning. "Your Highness?" Something about the way she said it made it sound like an insult. "How delightful to see you again. And so soon! To what do I owe this unexpected pleasure?"

He didn't wait for an invitation to assume the chair across her desk. "You know why I'm here." He unbuttoned his suit coat and crossed his legs, leaning back in the chair to lengthen his body.

"I can only assume you intend to pass yourself off as an investigator and snoop around. A little friendly advice, though: eventually, you're going to cross paths here with someone else besides me who knows who you really are, and then your cover is going to be blown."

It hadn't slipped his notice how she cataloged him, as though she contemplated his acquisition. Francisco, of course, had no interest in Tybor's acting director, but he wasn't above some harmless encouragement to get what he was after. "There's been another bombing outside of the war zones in GAIA. This time, two avatars were destroyed, and mine was one. So, I ask you the same question that I did before."

She folded her arms over her chest and gave him her undivided attention. "And my answer is the same. Or did you think I was lying?"

"You, lie?" Francisco chuckled and swiped the air. "I'm sure you don't think that's what I'm suggesting."

"So, you finally believe that I don't have access to the source code? Good. Not a single person in this building does."

"That right there, Johanna." Francisco snapped and pulled himself to the edge of his chair. "*That* is the kind of hedged comment that lets you skate around the truth, isn't it? *No one in this building.* Do you know what that makes me think about? About how long it's been since anyone's seen Rex Tieg at the office."

He'd plucked a string with that move, made Johanna Tieg buzz. The blonde placed two hands on the desk and methodically pushed herself back, standing slowly.

"Just to clarify, Your Highness, are you suggesting that my husband is a cyberterrorist using knowledge he's denied having to destroy Tybor's gift to humanity, that he's enabling such evil, or merely that I'm lying about his having such knowledge?"

"How could he *not* know about the source code?" Francisco demanded. "Wasn't Tybor and GAIA the result of his work with Omala Grover? Given the fact that they were married at the time, I find it hard to believe he's completely in the dark."

The momentary ghost of past grudges and insecurity erupted onto Johanna's face. As quickly as it came, it fled. The wrinkles around her eyes grew deeper as she pulled on a smile and sharpened her good graces. She rounded her desk with deliberate steps.

"I don't often share my personal feelings with anyone other than my husband, and on occasion, my own children. I hope you understand that, as I'm about to tell you something I've never shared with anyone else."

The prince acknowledged her with a dip of his chin. "Enlighten me."

"I detest GAIA."

The comment took him aback, both mentally and physically. "Why?"

"I could say because maintaining its infrastructure and hardware is a nightmare, both logistically and financially. How its bandwidth eats up precious resources I'd rather dedicate to our for-profit endeavors. Or, I could tell you that playing host to the world's most advanced war rooms makes us the constant target of hackers and shadow players. All these things are true, of course, but I'm afraid the real answer is very petty. I hate GAIA because it was *hers*. Because forever more, all the work I do will benefit the creation of the woman who, even fifteen years after her death, my husband still loves, no matter how much he denies it. I would rather it died, and with it, the

84

constant reminder Rex deals with of just how wonderful his ex-wife was."

She meant it. God help him, but she meant every word.

"And despite all this," Johanna continued, "I keep it going. I diminish our profit margins, skive from our investors, and raise billions of dollars a year in charity drives, to keep it going, because when it dies, I'm afraid my husband's heart—and our marriage—will die with it."

She settled back into her chair, leaning her forehead into hands pressed as if in prayer. When her closed eyes flew open again, Johanna reengaged her mask of slighted malevolence.

"Rex doesn't know how to access the source code, your majesty, and neither do I. No one knew except for Omala. As much as I detested her, I'm not bitter enough to say she was a fool, or to deny her genius. If there's someone, somewhere, who can get to the code, I haven't been able to find them. And so, I live each day in castles built of sand, knowing that someday, what we've built on top of Omala's work will collapse. For now, I'm just as determined to weed out whoever is attacking inside of it as you are."

And there it was. She'd tipped her hat. And now, Francisco had to decide if he'd do the same. Despite having no doubt that her admission had been true, he still wasn't certain her passion for the vreal world platform he ruled was as steadfast and compassionate as she claimed. But if he wanted her help, she needed to understand what he knew.

"I've made a discovery inside GAIA, Johanna."

The way curiosity pushed wide her eyes suggested intrigue.

"Accidentally, but nonetheless. There's a path between it and The Kingdom. I think...I think whoever is attacking us from inside GAIA is getting to us from there."

Johanna clutched the gold chain at her throat. "That's impossible. They're two completely different systems with the highest security protocols in the industry."

"But they run on the same source code."

"Yes, but...Your Highness, that's just not how it works."

"Why wouldn't it? Even if it's true, as you say, that hackers have never managed to get into GAIA, I know some have gotten into The Kingdom through the years. Don't talk to me like I don't understand this stuff." Francisco shot to his feet, looking down at the woman. "You know who I am."

"Yes, Prince Francisco Batista de le Reina, grandson of Martin Batista de la Leon, the man who funded Omala Grover's first iteration of GAIA."

"You also know that I studied vreal world design and architecture with some of the best teachers in the world, and I put myself through pirate port after pirate port to learn. I didn't win my crown just because of my family connections."

"You seem to think I'm your enemy. I'm not, and I have just as much to lose if word gets around about these events as you do. The Kingdom is a network of powerful and affluential people, each of whom vie mightily for access. There have only been three successful hacks in fifteen years, and we've crushed them and patched the weaknesses they exposed *immediately*. Even still, our stock tanked each time it happened, and took months to recover. GAIA is built on the same security protocols and framework. If word gets out that someone's not only hacking into it, but actually destroying parts, it will ruin Tybor."

Left hanging in the air between them: the destruction of GAIA, and all that implied. Francisco's hand absently went to his father's watch.

"Then give me your user records like I asked the first time."

"Absolutely not," Johanna snapped. "Our clients expect us to honor their privacy. Our product is one where they can act without judgement or reprimand. They do things inside they'd never commit in the real world, but that they wouldn't want getting out. You used to know that, or have you forgotten?"

It had been the years when Francisco was younger, more foolish. Not saddled with the legacy of a father slain before his eyes.

"Yes, we got up to all kinds of debauchery, but overthrowing the world government? I don't remember anything that extreme." It took a moment for the comment Johanna made to snap in his nets, but when it did, the fish was too big to throw back. "How open are the users with each other about who they really are these days?"

The change in subject and tone was so fluid, Johanna found herself thrown for a loop. "It varies, of course. Very few avatars are fully modeled on the client's true self."

The subtext of her passive aggressive comment, namely, *they're all not as foolish as you*, hit him, but Francisco let it go. He'd litigated that decision with far too many, most with more convincing arguments than anything Johanna would throw at him, and it still hadn't changed his mind.

"Kaylie knows the ones who frequent the Palace," she continued. "I have complete access to all user profiles and make it a point to know everyone worth knowing."

"Which is why you're the Queen." Francisco grinned as the image of a chess board overlaid the space between them in his mind's eye. Then, more to himself, he said aloud, "I wonder if that's knowledge you would ever share."

Johanna smirked right back, leaning into her coo. "Under the right circumstances. We are both royalty in our own way, after all, and royals have been... *coming* to understandings for eons."

Francisco leaned forward, running the middle finger of his right hand in a slow, laborious arc on Johanna's desk. "If the Gaian prince were to enter The Kingdom, would some be forthcoming? Letting me know who they truly are?"

"Particularly the young women, I'd imagine." Johanna suddenly came up to speed with where Francisco was heading, and the seduction play turned into fury. "Absolutely not! You think you can go into The Kingdom and lure the anarchists into the open? Do you want explosions going off in my palace, too? You can't squash those kinds of events there like you've been able to do with GAIA. Do you have any idea what that would do to our reputation?"

"Don't be silly, I don't want explosions," Francisco retorted. "The whole point of this is to end the violence going on in my capital. But to do that, I'm going to have to find the person hiding in yours."

"No one hides in my kingdom," Johanna said. "The consequences are too great."

"That's what I'm planning on." Francisco clapped as he rose to his feet. "Put out the word to your most prominent users, Tieg. The prince will be hosting a ball in three days at the Palace, and he wants to party. It's time I reacquaint myself with who these 'Kingdom people' are. And it's time for them to understand the kind of man I've become."

Fifteen

When she'd woken up to a talking mouse, Cindira considered that she might still be dreaming. Now, as she looked at the pair of transparent shoes in her hands and tried to believe they represented a nearly mythical high-tech device, the dream theory gained considerable traction.

"I don't understand." She held the right shoe to the light, seeing a clear, if slightly bent vision of the wall on the other side. "How could these possibly be jumpers? There's nothing in them."

"Your mother preferred to call them *slippers*, miss." The mouse scurried up Cindira's sleeve, perching itself on her shoulder. "I think because she could use them to *slip* inside GAIA from anywhere. And, although you can't see it, there's circuitry a plenty in there. She managed to use…"

"Nanites." Cindira completed the mouse's sentence as the thought occurred to her in parallel. "But I thought research into them was abandoned years ago."

"Outlawed, actually."

She turned her eyes on the mouse, a difficult thing to do with him so close to her face. "These are illegal?"

"Only if anyone finds out about them."

Guilt gnawed at her, pushing her to admit that, in fact, someone did know about them. But Kaylie had more or less dismissed the shoes, hadn't she? And if she'd known they contained illegal technology, she certainly would have no hesitation in using it to her advantage.

Or taking them for herself.

"You must make sure to keep that from happening," Laporte continued. "Even your father was not aware of your mother's work in this area. It was privately funded outside of Tybor. Their development was carried out in a restricted lab off the grid."

"You're telling me my mom had a secret life."

"A *private life*, actually, though I know the concept of that seems an anathema in these times. Omala didn't believe anyone was entitled to anything in her head or her heart. You and I are the only ones she truly opened up with, and in both cases, with restrictions due to our particular shortcomings."

When Cindira's face fell, Laporte developed a humanlike ability to correct himself.

"That was a poor choice of words, Madame. What I mean is, you were still a child when she died. In time, I'm certain she would have shared all her secrets with you, but of course you weren't ready back then. Likewise, while I've been programmed with a certain ability to understand and react to human emotions, at the end of the day, I am still a machine. My ability to be a confidante has its limits."

Like the shoes, this revelation bent the shape of her memories. Even though her mother had died while Cindira was in middle school, she still felt a kinship with the woman — uncommon for one of her age. It was almost as if the two were sisters rather than parent and child — though Omala could and did shift into an authoritarian roll at will. Rarely. No, they had a comradery. Nevertheless, she'd always known there were things her mother kept hidden. Or perhaps better to say, *reserved*. Cindira had had no doubts that as she grew older, she too would be let into the fantastical worlds her mother walked, both in reality and vreality.

They'd simply never gotten the chance.

Cindira resumed her study of the glass slippers. "I'm not even sure I need these. I was able to hack into GAIA simply enough."

"Technically, you didn't *hack* into anything. You logged into a parallel holding room for which you had anachronistic privileges and a waiting host profile."

Her heart quickened when she remembered that her mother's avatar still lay on that bed. "It's not gone, is it? Our apartment in GAIA?"

"No, Madame, though I just stated, that apartment is not *in* GAIA." The mouse blinked a few times. "You used to be so much more able to follow these discussions. Your understanding of code and structure has diminished without my tutelage."

"You're very conceited for an AI entity." *But to stay on task...* "I get what you're saying, but what I'm getting at is, if these were designed for GAIA, what makes you think I'll be able to use them for The Kingdom?"

"Because it's GAIA's source code laced over with far too many cosmetic layers. Your father and Johanna could never break into the source code themselves, but that didn't mean they couldn't make a clone of it. Probably they thought by putting it on servers that Omala didn't have access to, and instituting a new lattice of security measures, they could keep her out. They didn't realize that your mother had foreseen the possibility that someone might build another world without her authorization. She built doors into the source code. That same door your mother walked through to get into GAIA can just as easily walk into The Kingdom, or any other platform Tybor creates using her work."

"A door that can open into both platforms?" She remembered watching the prince meander through her step-sisters vreal world bedroom. "And are these shoes – the *slippers* – the only way to open that door?"

As much as the mouse could, he nodded. "The only way."

Well, there went that bubble of a theory.

But she wasn't going to think about it right now. No doubt the prince had resources aplenty, hackers and crackers, ways of getting around security measures. Right now, she needed to focus on the topic at hand. Or, Cindira thought as she looked at the slippers, at *feet*.

"How do they work?"

The mouse blinked twice. "You put them on."

"That's it?"

"No, but if you'll forgive the pun, that's the first step. And they must be worn without any interface. No socks, I'm afraid."

Just like the Indian-styled footwear her mother had preferred. Cindira laid the slippers on the floor and took a seat in preparation, pulling off her own everyday shoes. "And after I put them on, do they turn on somehow? Do I have to voice-command them?"

"They wouldn't be a covert device if you had to noticeably interact with them."

"But you have to, you know..." With fingers spread wide, her hands mixed the air. "I mean, a jackpod is designed to be laid down in, in part for safety. Even though the neural interface reads and writes to the brain, the physical body occasionally moves in response to mental stimuli. I don't exactly remember my mother taking lots of naps."

"No, but she did daydream quite a bit, didn't she?"

No sooner had Cindira opened her mouth to argue the statement than a cascade of memories came down over her. That distant look her mother would often have, her quiet moments of passivity which Cindira wrote off as "deep thinking." Omala had been a genius, after all, and an innovative mind was given to wander. She knew this from personal experience.

"She was inside of GAIA?"

"Your mother had a few secure points of entry in various locations around the platform," Laporte acknowledged. "Ones that were hidden from view and let her peak in for a few moments at a time when she wanted—or needed—to."

"But what about her avatar?" Cindira asked. "How did she show up at a specific location if her avatar is in our apartment even now?"

"An avatar is nothing but code, and even a world as complex as GAIA, nothing more than a vast array of programming and algorithms. For most users, the avatars are put away in a VR equivalent of a file. But your mother's avatar was stored at the root directory. It meant she could drill down anywhere she wanted. In time, you may learn to do the same." Laporte's head tilted to the side. "While the topic has been breached, Madame, can we discuss the destruction of your childhood avatar in the explosion?"

"Not really sure there's much to discuss. It was there, now it's not. Probably just as well, since I'm twenty-six, and it was still eleven."

"Be that as it may, it leaves you without a place to land when you try to jack in. We'll need to design you a new avatar, and soon. There are things going on inside that I'm having a hard time accounting for. Things which may make better sense to human eyes."

She put the shoes down and stood. "If it's an avatar I need, I'm going to have to go to Tybor. I don't have resources to create that here."

Which begged the question, where had her mother done all this stuff? Laporte had mentioned an off grid lab? When she'd turned twenty-one, all of Omala's papers and belongings, held in trust by her father, reverted to her. There wasn't much to it all—especially not after fifteen years in the proxy possession of Johanna Tieg. Most of the money was gone. Had probably been the first thing to go. A few dozen boxes of household and personal affects still sat in a storage locker in Oakland. She'd gone through it once but didn't recall coming across anything suggesting a clandestine life her mother her led under everyone's nose.

All things she'd need to bring up and discuss with Laporte, once she knew that she could trust him.

And that she wasn't, in fact, dreaming all this.

"I'd suggest waiting until you'd normally attend to your duties there; with your recent actions, if a spotlight catches a toe, they'll want to illuminate the whole body of your activities. Don't do anything outside your normal routine. As your friend Scotia would say, 'act cool.'"

Her eyebrow shot up. "You know Scotia?"

"I know *of* Scotia, attended several of her lectures on vreal world addiction and treatment. She truly is a gifted researcher."

"Fine," Cindira huffed. "I'll wait until my shift tomorrow to do anything. And what about you? Are you, like, my little sidekick now?"

"I'd prefer to think that I am assuming the place in your life I once held for your mother. I am your spy, as well as your assistant. Unless you'd prefer otherwise, I'd like to accompany you. But if I may ask one accommodation?"

Cindira dipped her chin. "Sure, what?"

"That you hide Asla's broom. She's nearly smashed me twice."

sixteen

Cindira blacked out the screen at her workstation as Kaylie unexpectantly entered the Kitchens.

Damn, she wished there was a place other than under the nose of her step-sister that she could handle this kind of work. Any kind of work. Humility was for the forgotten; Cindira knew she was the best coder the company had. One of the best in the world, frankly. But her talents were useless without the tools to practice them, and Tybor held control over them all. It was like being a master sculptor, but without access to clay and marble.

Hiding her new project, a brand-new avatar for herself, from her coworkers had been simple enough. It wasn't the first time she'd undertaken building a profile from scratch; her superior coding skills meant Johanna often assigned Cindira the task for the clients who agreed to pay the hefty fees (not that Cindira herself ever saw an additional cent for her labor.) The others were busy with assignments of their own and didn't notice the meek woman on Cindira's screen had begun to look more like a reflection than a rendition.

Generally, only celebrities whose brand was heavily tied up in their image designed avatars to look like their real-world selves, and Cindira was hardly a celebrity. A fleeting thought dashed across her mind: Her real-world self was her avatar. *This* couldn't possibly be her true self.

"Oh, good, you're here." Her stepsister lingered at the corner of her desk.

Act cool. "I do work here, Kaylie." Frustration made her snippy, it seemed. She'd had so little experience with it, and Kaylie even less with being on the receiving end, that it made both women pause and take on awkward expressions.

"Yeah, well, anyway..." Kaylie blinked. "Stop whatever it is you're doing. I need a new dress."

Cindira pointed back over her shoulder. "I saw a sale at McCarran's on my way in."

"What? No, not a dress! I mean a *dress dress*, for The Kingdom!"

"Another one?" Was the previous week set on replay? "I just made you one, then tweaked it even more."

"Right, and now I need another one."

Even for Kaylie, two custom-made dresses in as many weeks seemed excessive. "Why so soon? I'm sure there's still plenty of men who haven't seen you out of the other one."

Kaylie ate the insult with a great deal of effort. "There's a ball, and I need a new gown."

"There's a ball every night in The Kingdom."

"Yes, but not ones attended by the prince."

"The prince?" That got her attention. "The Gaian prince?"

Kaylie rolled her eyes. "What other prince do you know?"

"There's one in Sweden, Catalonia, Japan... I think that Bahrain still has a..."

"Yes, the Gaian prince!" Kaylie snapped. When her outburst drew the gazes of the other workers in the room, she brought herself back under control, though her words picked up speed and gruffness as she continued. "Prince Francisco has decided to reach out to the members of The Kingdom community to increase awareness of opportunities available to the wealthy to help the poor and destitute nations of the world, the ones who count on GAIA to mediate their problems. He's going to host a ball at the Palace tomorrow night and everyone important is invited."

A throbbing tick started to increase in both tempo and volume. After a few moments, Cindira realized it was her own pulse pounding in her ears. So, the prince was holding a ball. But why would such a high-profile personality jump into a platform known as a scandalous playground of the rich and famous? And how had he gotten into Kaylie's room? If she was going to figure out what he was up to, she needed to be where he was.

"I want to go."

"You want to..." Kaylie threw back her head and laughed.

"*You*, at the prince's ball? Don't be silly. You don't even have an avatar. What are you going to do, craft a whole new profile overnight? Please, Cindira, the process takes days!"

Not if you know Purasha and you're really, really good at coding. "It wouldn't take too long if I just used a digital scan of myself as a template. It wouldn't have to be anything fancy."

"Yes, it would," Kaylie insisted. "Eloquence – or *fancy*, as you call it – is part of our branding for that platform. It's all about the luxe, the fairytale, the overly-romanticized idea of a world of wonder and magic. You can't go into The Kingdom with some half-baked avatar, glitching all over the place and disgusting users who pay through the nose for exclusive access! It's an idealized landscape, Cindira, not a horror flick simulation! Besides, if you spend all your time scrapping together a new avatar from scratch before tomorrow night, then who would make my dress?"

"Any number of etailors." She didn't mean for the answer to sound snippy, but it was hard to fold it into any other shape. Like it or not, she'd never be able to make herself an avatar without Tybor's resources, and Kaylie was now her boss. When Kaylie shot daggers at her, Cindira found herself crumbling. "Fine, you're right. I just...I dreamed for a moment."

Kaylie savored the taste of her small victory, grinning. "I thought I had finally cured you of that habit."

Sometimes I wonder. "What color do you want?"

"Blue for me. Mother wants dark purple, and Cade would like you to design a suit for him that compliments both."

Cindira's eyes went wide. "*Three* new projects by tomorrow afternoon?"

"By tomorrow *morning*," Kaylie amended. "We'll need a chance to try them on and make any adjustments before we leave for the ball."

It might as well be three hundred. "I'm good, Kaylie, but I'm not that good. You...I couldn't possibly make three new projects from scratch in twenty-four hours."

And have any hope of fixing up an avatar for myself.

"Do, or don't. Your choice. But an employee who can't meet deadlines might not have a job if she fails to meet them."

Cindira leaned back. "This isn't part of my job."

"Isn't it?" Kaylie sneered. "Are you not the lead code writer on the customization division? Are you not receiving a direct order from your supervisor?"

"But, Kaylie, I—"

"Enough!" The blonde clapped her hands in Cindira's face, cutting off her words. "Mother, Cade, and I will meet you tomorrow in the Sink to inspect your work. Now, get busy."

Cindira collapsed back into her chair in the wake of Kaylie's departure, her forehead falling against fingertips pressed into her temples. Never mind the fact the she herself was going to miss the ball, the perfect opportunity to get close to the prince without any of his usual security detail and figure out what was really going on inside of GAIA. Now, on top of that, she'd be working overnight just to get the clothing programmed.

She stirred when she felt a hand on her shoulder. Cindira turned her head up to find that one of her junior coders, a mousy woman whose name she couldn't recall, staring down at her with a tender smile. Behind her, the dozen other coders on duty flanked her.

"Don't worry, Miss Tieg," the soft voice cooed. "We'll help you."

seventeen

Kaylie strode into view, her gown so diaphanous, its voluminous ivory skirting made her appear to walk through rolling mist. Such had been the intention of the design, and to Cindira's delight, her vision had been realized.

Just because she didn't want the work didn't mean she couldn't take pride in it.

Her stepsister extended an arm, examining the complex silver stitchery on her sleeve. "You're certain this wasn't just pulled out of some old file? Seems very detailed for something thrown together in a day."

Cindira labored to suppress her ire as she pushed the button on the control panel that let her voice be heard in Kaylie's vreal world bedroom. "Every single thread is newly programmed. I've cross-referenced against all the other gowns that have been uploaded to client libraries in the last three days since the ball was announced. This dress is by far the most elegant and the most complex."

"And the color?" Kaylie looked up as though looking in a mirror. "I've never worn white in The Kingdom before. Does it suit me?"

Nearby, Mackey fixed a hungry gaze on the boss lady. "I'll say."

"Shhh!" Cindira pressed a finger to a smile she couldn't hide. As soon as the others quieted their own giggles, she opened the channel again. "It's not white precisely." *It would be misadvertising if I put you in something suggesting you were pure.* "It has a tinge of blue in it, enough to shade it. The Kingdom's lighting algorithms don't treat pure white well. It confuses it for translucent, and I've even heard reports that sometimes it looks like the user's clothing disappears."

A wily, cocky half-grin pulled up a corner of Kaylie's mouth. "That doesn't sound like an entirely unwelcome glitch, but not right for tonight."

Time for the upsell. The last thing Cindira wanted to

admit to was that she and the other coders had decided a mostly monochromatic palette would make their jobs easier. Color created complexity. "I modeled your dress after old videos of the marine layer. *You* will roll into the room, blanketing out everything else so that the only thing anyone sees when they turn in any direction is your presence."

"And I'll leave them feeling wet."

Cindira bit her tongue on that.

"So...?" She drew out the word and her hopes, waiting for judgement.

Kaylie huffed and let her arms fall to the side. "It will have to do, I suppose."

Cindira's hope for even the slightest bit of appreciation evaporated.

Kaylie appeared to be looking right at them, even though it was impossible for her to see the Kitchens from inside The Kingdom. "You're going to turn off this mirror contraption when I leave, right? I don't want any of you spying into my bedroom later. I *may not* be alone."

In her own bedroom? Whenever Kaylie had undertaken one of her virtual hookups before, it was outside of Alsace. *Not* that the two women shared intimate details of their love lives, or if they had, that Cindira would have had anything to share. The men in whom Kaylie took interest were wealthy enough to have their own mansions, and going to their place was easier and safer than having Cindira upgrade the security setting on the profile of her *beau du jour*. Not to mention, she shared the space with her mother and brother. Even inside virtual reality, how creepy would that be? That Kaylie planned to have a guest without such concerns meant only one thing.

"You've already given the prince security clearance for Alsace?" Cindira asked.

"Of course, I did," Kaylie snipped back. "He doesn't have a residence in The Kingdom for us to go to, does he? The only place for me to have him would be for him to *come* here."

Kaylie Fife rarely let an entendre go undoubled.

Cindira pushed the mic button again. "Aren't you scared you'll be interrupted?"

The fact that Kaylie didn't answer told Cindira all she needed to know. This wasn't just another virtual conquest for Kaylie. This plan had larger implications, ones that, no doubt, Johanna was part of.

But those all depended on the prince buying in, and that he'd be into someone like Kaylie. The flirtation his Highness had shown during his visit as Detective Batista fled the moment he understood Kaylie couldn't give him what he was after. Who was to say that hasn't changed though?

In the back of her mind, Cindira wondered what the prince would make of a quiet, brainy girl instead.

"We'll shut down the window right after you leave. I'm the only one from the Kitchens who has clearance to enter Alsace, and I won't be here much longer."

A smile teased Cindira's voice.

"Cade and my mother say they find their outfits acceptable, so I suppose we're done here. Close the window." Kaylie grabbed a matching handbag off the table next to her. "I'm off to the ball."

No sooner had Kaylie stepped out of view and presumably, left the room, then Cindira whipped around to her team. They deserved her praise. They deserved her thanks. They deserved her appreciation and recognition. The deserved a bottle of wine and the rest of the night off.

All things she'd have to give them later.

"I really hate to do this, but I have to go."

eighteen

"I still don't have an avatar." Cindira slung her backpack over her shoulder as she shot out of the Kitchens. "Not sure how I'm pulling this off without that."

Laporte emerged from his hiding spot, a zippered pocket on the front of the bag, and crawled up to perch upon Cindira's shoulder. "You *do* have an avatar."

"No, it was destroyed in an explosion, remember?" T*hough even if it hadn't, wouldn't it freak out Batista to see me approaching him?* "I'd barely gotten the wireframes on the replacement drawn yesterday when Kaylie came in about her stupid dress."

"It was a beautiful dress, though, Madame."

"You have to stop calling me 'Madame,' Laporte. It's Cindira."

"Yes, Miss."

Well, at least it didn't make her feel like a brothel owner.

The mouse continued. "When she diverted you from your task, I was forced to find a solution."

Cindira stopped dead in her tracks. "What? How?"

"I took the liberty of preparing a render very similar to your real-world representation." He kept silent for a moment, except that so close to her ear, Cindira swore there was some sort of high-pitched tone coming from inside him. "Your family has left Alsace. It is now safe for you to use it is a port entry undetected."

"I wish there was a better place to get in."

"As you yourself had said, it is the only port of entry in the area which won't trigger an arrival record. Ideally, you'd enter through the magic pumpkin, but as I've noted, its entrance point to The Kingdom is very far from the Palace."

"Couldn't you just edit the entry logs?" She reached the room she'd been heading for, the only one she could think of where no one would come in to find her. Not even the custodian had access to Kaylie's new office. Cleaning staff were only allowed in with the division head present. Cindira had been granted access by Kaylie herself, "just in case I ever need you to do something for me when I'm not here."

"I have access to the source code, Miss, but all the structure that Tybor has built into The Kingdom since its inception is beyond my influence. I can only read the files, not overwrite them."

After fifteen years, Cindira had discovered the first flaw in her mother's work. She ducked into the office, locking the door behind her before throwing her bag on Kaylie's desk. Inside, the glass slippers clinked, despite having been wrapped in kitchen towels.

"I swear, I'm going to break these things."

"Highly unlikely, miss. Your mother used metallic glass. It's nearly indestructible."

"You don't know what I'm capable of." She set the slippers on the floor, aligned them with her feet, before slipping her shoes and socks off and stuffing them in the bag. "You said it's best if I lay down until I get used to using them, just in case. I guess I can do that here on the floor, but are you sure this isn't going to, like, fry my brain?"

"No, it will not 'fry your brain.'" The mouse's tone managed to be mocking despite his inability to have true emotions. "Once you put them on, they will need about thirty seconds to boot up and acclimate to your neural signals."

"They read my brain waves through the soles of my feet? Is it safe? Is it painful?"

"Miss Tieg, now is not the time. I assure you, it's safe. I will send the command for the devices to jack you into The Kingdom when you're ready."

Cindira fixed the slippers in her gaze, then looked at her bare feet, then the slippers again. Either she was going to do this, or she wasn't.

She drew in a breath, closed her eyes, and lifted her right foot.

And then came the knock on the door.

Three quick taps sent her pulse spiraling as Laporte turned towards the entry.

"I think that would be Miss MacAvoy."

"Oh my god, the invitation!" Cindira ignored the shoes and rushed to the other side of the room. "I almost forgot."

Laporte had scrambled out of view by the time Cindira had collected herself enough to open the door. When she did, it was only to crack it wide enough to press her face into view.

"Scotia, thank you for coming."

The redhead narrowed her gaze, suspicion taking hold of her features. "What's going on? Why am I meeting you at Kaylie's office, and why aren't you opening the door?" She curled up on her tippy toes, trying to see over her friend's head. "What are you hiding in there?"

"Why would you think I'm trying to hide something?"

"Because you won't let me see inside?" The redhead fell back to her heels and cocked a hip. "What's up with you? You show up at my house in the middle of the night after saying you'd blown up the prince of GAIA, then disappear the morning after without so much as a goodbye. Then, I don't hear from you until this morning when you send a message begging to use my invitation to the Ball."

As a prominent researcher in the community, Scotia was often pulled into appearing at larger events – even if just for political reasons.

"You're right. I am sorry I took off like that, and I should have reached out earlier to thank you. I promise, I'll make it up to you. And I swear, I'm not trying to keep something from you, but for the moment, I have to. It has... *had* something to do with my mom."

All true, and all things she didn't have time to go into further at the moment.

"Do you have it?"

Scotia raised her comque and clicked a few screens. Soon enough, the projection of a rectangular invite inscribed in archaic artist script hovered a few inches above her wrist. "You do realize all the credentials went out yesterday, and if you didn't RSVP by this morning, the invitation was revoked."

"I can alter the coding to change that. It just has to scan as valid when I enter the Palace."

"It won't do any good," Scotia argued. "If the credential doesn't match your profile when midnight hits, you're still going to be kicked out."

"That's more than enough time."

Scotia grimaced. "To do what?"

Cindira bit her bottom lip, a series of consequences spinning in her mind. None of the possible results seemed worse than lying to her best friend. "It's the only way I can think of to talk to the prince."

"The prince?" Scotia repeated. "Why would you need to talk to him? Is it about what happened when you were inside GAIA? Hey, didn't you say your avatar was destroyed? Did you make... Where are you going?"

Cindira looked past her guilt to remember the truth: she was stepping into risky territory, and any knowledge she gave her best friend would only place her in danger.

"I'm sorry, Scotia, I really am. But I can't tell you anymore. Thank you for giving me your invitation. Thank you for *everything*, but I really have to go."

With the door locked and without any further delay, Cindira stepped into the glass slippers. If she had been expecting anything miraculous to happen from that fact alone, she was severely disappointed. The only novel exception was that she now knew from experience that shoes made of metallic glass were as comfortable as they sounded. Namely, not.

She laid back on the floor. "Now what?"

Laporte laid down by her right hand. "Just close your eyes and dream."

nineteen

The sunset consumed the horizon, painted it in extravagant reds bursting with orange hues. Brilliant, blinding colors danced across her eyelids, burning her retinas with the most delicious tease. Cindira blinked, sitting up, taking her first look at a world her mother had unwittingly created. The light broke in from a square-paned window, and even as she sat up, the angle of the sunbeam pitched as the sun set outside. She was in Alsace, her step-mother's home inside The Kingdom. In the front parlor, from what she could tell. The plush fabric of the Persian rug beneath her felt so real as she pushed herself up to a seated position. The full-immersion experience proved much richer than just tinkering in The Sink.

Only then did she become aware of the stiff, itchy fabric scratching her legs.

"What am I wearing?"

The unflattering skirt looked more like an oversized towel she'd wrapped around and tucked at the waist. It came down to her ankles; a starched, white pinafore stretched nearly as far. The billowing blouse appeared to be made of gingerbread-colored gingham. On her head, white linen that came together in under her chin and melded seamlessly into a long collar that covered her chest, shoulders, and upper back. A veil? A nun's habit? She couldn't remember anyone saying the prince's ball would be a masquerade.

Cindira inspected herself with concern. "This isn't a ballgown."

Something had happened to her voice. It held a bit of an accent, perhaps? Which, she couldn't quite place, but something about it proved familiar, comforting. *Part of the fantasy*, she thought. Whatever made the world more enticing, thus, more addicting, Tybor labored to achieve.

Laporte sounded like he was right next to her, though she couldn't see him anywhere.

"Your task is better achieved by avoiding notice rather than drawing it. I know we had discussed choosing a random dress from those in The Kingdom libraries left unused tonight, but I thought I

105

might first present my argument for donning a servant's garb instead."

"If the point is to avoid attention, then I should be in a gown. I'm going to stand out dressed like this."

She stood, and immediately stopped in place. It wasn't that the costume was uncomfortable, even if a little over done with the weight of the cloth. But the shoes? No servant would ever wear something so impractical.

Cindira pulled up the skirt and found what she feared. "I'm still wearing the glass slippers?"

"It is one design flaw, Miss. Your mother was brilliant, but even she made mistakes. While one is jacked into the vreal world wearing the slippers, they will also render on the avatar once logged in. I apologize there is nothing to be done for it. I think your mother may have intended it to be some sort of indication of authority. If so, she never shared it with me."

The code writer took a few steps to test their feel. "They're not as awkward here as they are in the real world. And they don't make any noise?"

"You can also change the shape while you're here. If you'll notice, I've had the shoes rendered as flats, which match the wardrobe."

Annoying, but workable. Cindira adjusted the pinafore. It hadn't been an impromptu job; even if the clothing appeared mundane, as a virtual object, the rendering was to be admired. She couldn't detect any pixilation, and the contours of her form had been well and realistically rendered. As she looked down at herself, she slid her hand over the rise of her hip bone. *Exceptionally well rendered,* she thought.

"Where did the design for this outfit come from?"

Still no body, only Laporte's voice. "It is the design worn by the NPC servants in the Palace."

"The Non-Player Characters?" Cindira asked, performing a little QA of her own. "We call those VAPORs now." She pressed an index finger to the patch of skin between her eyes, finding that Laporte had given her a fake bhindi so she'd match the other bots. "I'm not a bot. Surely someone will realize that when they look at me."

"That's the key to it, Miss. In the Palace, very few users ever even notice an NPC—a VAPOR, if you prefer. That includes your step-mother and siblings."

"I guess that makes sense. Thanks, Laporte. Good thinking. Now, what's the best way to get to the Palace itself?"

"By coach, Miss. One is on its way now; it will meet us out in the main street in a few minutes. The credential Scotia transferred to you will get you onto the palace grounds. However, as Scotia herself mentioned, the midnight protocols will sweep you out when it sees you and has no record of your entry."

"I know. Only, if that's true, how does my family get away with it?" She broadened her search around the first floor, looking to see in which corner the little mouse had stuffed himself. "*Why* are you hiding?"

"I'm not hiding, miss. I'm just... Well..." His hesitance suggested contemplation, an internal debate. But that was impossible, wasn't it? Sure, Laporte's programming might encourage him to give emotional indicators, but it was just that... programming.

Finally, he continued. "In the real world, your mother decided to make me look like a mouse because rodents are both innocuous and a pest. No one would hesitate to swat me away, as Asla is so keen on doing. It also made my physical iteration very transportable. In the vreal world, however, there is no need for such considerations. Just remember that I can look like anything you want except a registered avatar, so if my current appearance doesn't suit, I can alter it."

"You mean you look different here?"

But why shouldn't he? After all, the vast majority of the players inside The Kingdom had avatars carefully tailored to be their ideal selves, whether that was getting rid of a bump on the nose, or by appearing slender and tone when the reality was anything but. Her step-sister had uncharacteristically gone against the trend. Kaylie's mods were skin deep. Literally. All her alterations had been performed in the real world; why change in the vreal one was had so perfectly been rendered in flesh? Not the mention, Kaylie had been a public figure not long after The Kingdom launched, her step-sister must have felt her face was already part of her brand, and thus her appeal.

Laporte didn't speak. Instead, the doorknob of a nearby closet turned and the door creaked open.

As a human, Laporte was utterly unremarkable, and even retained some of his mousier qualities. Although he appeared as a boy in his late teens or early twenties, he was of a diminutive stature, the top of his head on par with her chin. Black hair, black eyes, an unassuming boyish smile. In every way plain and by that virtue, non-threatening.

And somehow, familiar.

"Is this iteration to your satisfaction?" The voice was the same, however.

Cindira smiled and nodded. "Why wouldn't it be? Is this avatar modeled on someone from the real world?"

Someone my mother knew?

"I'm afraid I don't know." He approached, his hands laced behind his back. "My knowledge inside your mother's platforms is fairly comprehensive, but outside of that, I'm afraid highly lacking. I'd like to think she modeled me on a student she might have known once. Maybe even a teacher."

Laporte, the academic. Suiting, somehow.

"But we mustn't waste time speculating." He reached out and took her hand, pulling her toward the door. "The ball has already begun, and Yuchi will be suspicious if you arrive too late."

She let out a yelp as the mouse-turned-pageboy yanked on her arm a little too hard. Not that he could injure her, of course. One could experience pain inside the vreal world; it was neural feedback deemed necessary to render the experience authentic, but death, when it rarely occurred, was merely symbolic.

Laporte pasted on an apologetic smile. "Sorry, Miss Cindira."

"No harm done." They made it out the front door. "Who is Yuchi?"

"The security bot that guards the Palace."

In her mind, she visualized a sweet little Japanese woman well matched to the name, and the horrific yet funny prospect of watching such a woman dispense of trespassers.

"Only a certain level of paid clientele is permitted to enter," Laporte continued, "and tonight, those restrictions are even tighter. Yuchi makes sure that only those who are meant to be there, are there."

"Scotia's clearance is that high?"

Even from the side, she caught the young man's smile. "To be honest, I'm not certain if Miss MacAvoy is aware she's at such a high tier. The change to her profile was only recently requested by your brother, Cade."

"My *step-brother*, you mean. That explains it."

Had Cade extended the invitation to what was turning out to be the social event of the season, hoping to stroke Scotia's ego and woo her?

Whatever. She couldn't focus on that now. She needed to keep her mind on the obstacles to her goals. "Is it Yuchi that runs the midnight protocols?"

"Indeed, and I'm not too eager to get on his bad side."

Well, perhaps she should have imagined a little Japanese *man*.

twenty

Cindira had seen slips of The Kingdom before, even recognized passing elements of it as her own creation. But now, she could appreciate it in full. Here a flower in front of one of the luxurious mansions along the river, a combination of a red rose and a black tulip that held the petals of both. There a store front selling linens and dinnerware. (After all, if you were going to allow users to buy luxurious properties, they'd need to furnish and decorate them.) But to see it with her own eyes! Or at least, eyes that belonged to her. It was as though someone had hooked a 3D printer into her dreams and manufactured her visions in real time. Depth, texture... even the scent of roasting hazelnuts in the air had all her senses buzzing. The streets weren't empty, either. They bustled, full of women and men strolling, dressed in varying levels of baroque finery. There were even a few dogs and one man walking a monkey on a leash. Bots, of course. One couldn't jack a real animal into the vreal world; they didn't have the cerebral capacity for it.

Cindira wanted to order the coach to stop so she could get out and explore each inch in excruciating detail. Beside her on the bench sat Laporte, diminutive in stature and miniscule in concern.

He fished a piece of gold-leafed card stock from his pocket and handed it to her. "Here. This is the invitation Scotia transferred to you. I've rewritten the code to timestamp it as verified yesterday."

Her fingers indexed the bumps and crevices of the fine parchment, marveling in the experience. "It feels so real. How will this get me through? Yuchi will take one look at me dressed as a servant and know that something is wrong."

"The invitation itself is the key. You perceive it as paper, but all this really represents is a package of code, credentials."

She dipped her chin. "How did *you* get ahold of it?"

Laporte's face looked like a dam holding back a great weight of water. "Best if we not speak of it."

"Fair enough." She tucked the card into a pocket. "How deep does your knowledge go? Do you know where everyone is?"

The boy clicked his tongue. "I know who is signed in; when they pass into a new section of the program, I know that they are in *that* area. I don't know specifics beyond that. For example, I can tell you the prince, as well as your family, are currently in the Palace. But where in the Palace precisely? I don't know. To me, that information all looks the same."

A glimmer of an idea crept into the back of her brain. Maybe she wouldn't have to track down Batista at all. Maybe Laporte could simply tell her what she needed to know. "When someone's logged in, can you read their mind?"

Wide-eyed, the mouse-turned-man looked aghast. "Of course not. Your mother was adamant in my design and in the design of her platform that the user's mind would remain free of intrusion any more than was necessary to control its avatar. A wise human once said, 'knowledge is power.' Omala understood that and knew the first temptation of a creation such as hers would be to use it as a mechanism of intelligence. How would GAIA have saved the world, if it was simultaneously building the chains that would enslave it?"

For reasons she couldn't quite vocalize, Cindira felt ashamed of even asking. Before she could continue the topic, however, the road under the wheels of the coach turned from dirt to cobblestone, making their smooth ride into a bumpy, jostling nightmare.

"We've entered the palace grounds," Laporte said to her unasked question.

The piece of paper that she'd been holding blipped out of existence. "The invitation...it disappeared!"

"But you did not." He smiled as the coach began to slow and the discomfort abated. "That means it—and you—have been given a pass by Yuchi. The first hurdle is crossed."

Cindira pulled herself to the edge of the bench, peaking her head past the heavy curtained window just in time to see the backside of the palace gates. The archway was truly a marvel to behold. She'd read articles about it in VR architectural reviews, and knew it was modeled after the Habsburg Gate in the real world with one significant difference: the massive clock face set in the top or the arch. One of the early challenges in a VR environment had been deciding how time would work, and if there should be time at all. Cindira's mother had argued it was a constant in the real world, and the virtual one, and human mind, would falter without it. Unlike GAIA, The Kingdom moved in time with +0 GMT. The Baum Clock at the Palace measured time with computer precision, running eight hours ahead of San Francisco.

Cindira eased back into her seat. "What's the next hurdle?"

"You must find your prince."

The coach pulled to a stop at the back of the grounds. Laporte presented a hand, helping Cindira to step down safely, before ushering her into a room where a staff of several dozen worked a kitchen that looked like something from a period piece movie. All around, women dressed in identical wear went about their business. For a moment, Cindira worried they'd see her classifiers – her servant's garb—and assume she was one of them. To her surprise, however, none of them paid her the slightest mind.

"Are they all bots?"

Laporte surveyed the servants, then pointed to one man working at a distant table, folding pieces of pastry into edible origami. "The sous chef is from the real world. Bots can mix consistent, delicious recipes, but only a true chef can give them a human touch. In essence, he's here to make the meal perfect, by making it slightly *imperfect*."

"That's a contradiction."

"That's humanity," Laporte shot back.

No one took notice of them as they passed, a fact that both relieved and confused her. How far would she be able to make it into the Palace without the security bots realizing she wasn't who the invitation said she was? After a few minutes weaving through halls, the level of opulence rising with each turn like a set of river locks slowly filling and carrying the boat within higher, they came to circular vestibule where three intimating oak doors stretched from floorboards to crown molding.

"This is one of the pipelines," Laporte said, and as he continued he held up a hand to indicate each in turn from left to right. "The backroom, only accessible by décor bots and a limited number of Tybor avatars. When The Kingdom was being constructed without Omala's knowledge, it was from this point forward. The center door leads to the residential part of the Palace, though no one really lives here. It's called the Coeur. High-end users can rent out that portion for exorbitant fees, but only on a nightly basis. Think of it as a luxurious bordello. *They* do."

Her stomach curdled as she thought of the difference between all the good GAIA did, and all the malicious, indulgent activities that kept The Kingdom ticking.

Finally, Laporte extended a pointed finger to the last door. "That way eventually leads to the ballroom, and also the library, the dining rooms, the throne room, and eventually, the terraces and drives that connect the Palace with the rest of the kingdom. If you're looking for the prince, that is likely where you'll find him."

"But it's also where my family will be. I don't want Kaylie or Johanna to know I'm here. I hope you're right, that I blend in as a servant, but if they look straight at me, they're going to realize who I am."

"That's highly unlikely."

"Yeah, well, I wish I had your confidence." Cindira looked at each of the doors in turn. "If only there were a way for me to look for the prince without being in the room. God, I wish this world had electronics. I'd march a drone bug in there without thinking."

Laporte took in her side profile. "Miss Cindira, may I ask what it is you're hoping to accomplish here tonight?"

He asked the question like an AI entity would: simply, and as though the answer should be equally as simple. But like Laporte himself had said, humans were perfectly imperfect.

"I need to talk to the prince."

"To what end?"

Wasn't that the question? "I don't know if I can put it into words yet. Explosions in the Gaian capital being covered up? The prince sniffing around at Tybor? I need to know what's going on, if my mother's legacy is truly in danger. I know you don't understand what instinct is..."

"Instinct: noun. An innate, typically fixed pattern of behavior in animals in response to certain stimuli."

"Yes, but do you *understand* it? The prince feels like the way to fight whatever is going on in GAIA is by having access to the source code." She shook her head, as though she could shake away the fuzziness of what she was thinking. "Maybe it's as simple as the code breaking down after years of use without proper updates. If that's the case, fixing it may be simple enough. But I need to understand not only what's going on, but also what he's intending to do about it. I'm the only one who…"

The mouse looked at her with his human eyes full of hope. "You're the only one who can help." As suddenly as his pride had come over him, he masked it with reproach. "A fact that makes you the most dangerous person in The Kingdom."

"How?"

"Miss Tieg, you seem to be under the impression that GAIA is the platform which serves as the world's place for diplomacy and warcraft. It is the public face, I'll grant you that. But what you—and based on what you're saying, perhaps Prince Francisco—need to realize is that *this world* is where the money and power truly are. And they are growing weary of competition."

He pulled her towards the center door, which opened as though by magic upon their approach. "Come, there is one room in the residence from which you can see the ballroom below. Don't worry, it doesn't work the other way. You'll be safely hidden, and from there, you can get the full picture of what's really going on."

twenty-one

Kaylie Fife was in her natural habitat: the center of attention. Not for much longer, though. The Gaian prince had yet to show his face at the ball, but the moment Francisco Batista de la Reina did, all eyes would swing to him.

Like so many other elements of The Kingdom, the Palace's ballroom had been modeled on the height of classical European style, though at a scale that the architects of that era could never have imagined. Four stories high, no less than six glittering crystal chandeliers, each the size of a minibus, hung on golden chains from a ceiling covered in rich murals. Ivory-colored columns framed the walls, each topped by the gold-leafed bust of the human form in divine perfection. Under their feet: floors made with slabs of golden tile, interrupted at regular intervals with exquisite mosaics. The only things that outshone such exquisite design was the compliment of its company: titans of industry, masters of the arts, creators of culture (for whom the exuberant access fees were paid by "patrons," but whom most people called "sugars"), and the dirty, filthy, stinking rich. By requirement, the costumes matched the motif: ballgowns and fine suits cost a pretty penny to code, and it showed.

When the invitations had first gone out to the highest tier of kingdom society, many weren't sure what to make of it. GAIA generally kept to itself, and that's the way they preferred it. A prince had never revealed himself to the public prior to the end of his five-year term of office, his identity concealed to avoid approach by interested parties. The de facto world government created a convenient mask, and its actions and wars, a distraction on the wires each evening. Meanwhile, the true global power brokers came to The Kingdom, a dalliance of a platform that provided the backdrop for all they wanted to be done.

Francisco Batista hadn't revealed himself publicly, per se, but the fact that he'd created this event in order to, as the invitation had said, "make acquaintance with the patrons of our sister city," had everyone on edge. Everyone, that was, except Kaylie. As the daughter of Johanna Tieg, and a high-leveled manager at Tybor, she scoffed at the idea that GAIA could interfere with this land in which *she* ruled, socially if not actually.

And, if she played her cards right, even that would change.

"Good evening, Pet."

Pietro Mancusi slid her direction, his fine hips carrying a muscular frame she'd had the pleasure of inspecting at length only a week before. Dressed in a modern interpretation of baroque couture befitting the platform, he still managed to stand apart from the crowd with his good looks alone. She wasn't certain how much of his avatar was based on his real-world self; she'd been too scared of disappointment to make an occasion to see him there, despite several overtures. Not to mention, he lived in Italy, or what remained of it, and Rome simply was not in fashion these days.

"What a lovely gown." He placed a kiss across her knuckles. "I look forward to taking you out of it later."

She retracted her hand the moment he removed his lips. "Sorry, but I'm working tonight."

"Oh, dear." He feigned hurt, pushing a hand to his heart. "Does Mommy have you seducing senators again? Or perhaps a certain visiting dignitary?"

"Mr. Mancusi." Johanna chose just that moment to arrive, her blond hair pulled and pushed in such a twist of loops and weaves, it looked like an angry ocean. She laced her arm through Kaylie's, pulling the latter insistently to her side. "Would you mind, signore, if I borrowed Kaylie for a moment?"

Kaylie attempted an apology through a half-hearted grimace. She wasn't at all upset to be parted from so recent a beau. It was like eating at a fine restaurant; the experience and tastes were delightful, but one needed a sufficient space of time before another visit would be as appealing.

When they were far enough from the others, Johanna rounded.

"You are not here to randomly socialize."

"I know."

"And you are certainly not here to have one of your fairytale fucks."

Kaylie bit the inside of her mouth so hard that she'd have

116

tasted blood in the real world. "I know. I'm here to seduce royalty."

Johanna held the fury of a fire in her eyes. "Keep your eyes open. The second Francisco emerges, be on him like chips on silicon. Be certain he speaks only with those who wouldn't cause trouble for us later. And for god's sake, keep him from the Coeur. He might be intending to explore."

"You mean like he was exploring Tybor two weeks ago?" the blonde snapped at her mother. "I still can't believe you even let him in the door, almost as much as I can't believe that you waited until yesterday to tell me who he really was."

Johanna sneered. "The terms of a Non-Disclosure Agreement have always baffled you, haven't they?"

Before her daughter could protest, Johanna immediately jumped back in. "As for letting him in: I didn't have a choice. Tybor's agreements with the GAIA Congress allow the elected monarch unfettered access to our facilities. To have denied him would have caused more problems than it solved." Johanna turned her eyes across the dancefloor filled with swishing dresses and clicking heels, up past the grand staircase, to where a second, hidden staircase lay behind a secret door. "I can't risk anyone finding out about Rex."

The ire Kaylie had shown just moments ago dissipated as she focused on that covert space. "There's no change, then?"

Johanna shook her head. "And people are beginning to notice. Even Cindira is getting suspicious. If she finds out..."

"She won't." Her own troubles aside, Kaylie actually took a moment to think about the situation from her mother's perspective. "He can't stay like that forever, Mother. Pretty soon you'll need to..."

"If I can find no other remedy, I will," Johanna snapped. She brought her gaze back to her daughter. "I know my place, don't forget yours. Mind Francisco. Let's get through this charade without any surprises, okay?"

And in a swirl of purple silk, Johanna was gone, mixing back among the guests.

twenty-two

Cindira followed Laporte, despite the quick clip and regardless of how the unyielding material of her skirt made each step labored.

"I've never heard of the Coeur or Yuchi," she said as they came to a grand marble staircase and began to climb, her guide leading the way. "I thought I knew a lot about The Kingdom. Are there any other secrets I'm unaware of?"

"To know the answer to that question, Miss, I'd have to know what you know. Sadly, that is impossible."

She didn't think Laporte chose his words without purpose. "Sadly?"

"As I mentioned, I am not aware of the details of your mother's death. It happened during one of the few processes during which I'm unaware of what's going on in the real world."

She'd have to ask later if that was still true. That, even as he was here now in the avatar of a young man, his physical mouse iteration remained conscious back at Tybor, guarding her body. Though what a mouse could do to help was questionable.

Laporte continued, "I have a feeling that, if I were able to access your memories the way I can do with an artificial system, I might be able to find clues. Ones you may even be aware of but are unable to contextualize with your inferior human cognitive abilities."

The staircase narrowed as they reached the second floor and turned to ascend to the third. "Gee, Laporte, tell me what you really think."

"I don't say this to insult you, but it will not help our endeavors if you fail to remember my abilities and use them to your full advantage. I—"

Cindira harrumphed as she came crashing into Laporte's back. Confused, she lifted her head to see what had frozen her companion's movements.

The woman before them had black eyes. Not just pupils, but the entire orb. Like an animal's, and yet, far deeper than any other creature she had ever seen. She didn't conform to The Kingdom's Eurocentric, seventeenth century norms, dressed instead in the garb of ancient Japan, right down to a katana sword which she bore before her. The implied threat didn't go over Cindira's head: namely, if she advanced, that sword would go *through* Cindira's head.

Laporte regained his footing even as he took Cindira's hand and pulled her to the same step on which he stood. "Yuchi, how are you?"

"That's Yuchi?" She found herself whispering, then immediately wondered at the effort. "You said it was a guy."

"A bot doesn't have a consistent gender, but your language defaults to male pronouns. He, she... Yuchi can be either."

"Or neither." The accent vaguely matched the persona, making her somehow even more awe-inspiring. Yuchi kept her eyes trained on Laporte. "Third floor access is restricted to Tier Zero users. *You* know this."

Cindira huffed. "There is no such thing as Tier Zero users."

Only to be refuted by Laporte moments later. "She is a Tier Zero user. Check her credentials."

Anxiety twisted her insides. Wasn't avoiding detection by Yuchi one of the things they had said they wanted to accomplish?

Yuchi's eyes became distant for a moment, the inky black stained by dots of colors, all popping in and out of view with great rapidity.

"She *is* a Tier Zero user." Yuchi turned to Cindira, sheathing her sword. The bot bent at the waist. "You may pass, Miss Grover."

Cindira rushed past the samurai, even as she corrected by instinct, "It's Tieg, actually."

She'd changed it after she'd moved in with her father. Her mother's legacy gave a teenage girl working her way through academic circles too much baggage to tow.

"Negative." Yuchi twisted at the hip, even while keeping her feet planted. "User's name is Omala Grover."

119

So that's how he'd been able to get her in to The Kingdom, even though the new avatar she'd been creating for herself remained incomplete. Even as she turned, and with Yuchi between them, Cindira knew she'd just made a mistake. Laporte wore the evidence in his expression. Suddenly, a woman who didn't care too much for how the world observed her, wanted nothing more than a mirror.

Hands pressed to her face brought understanding. "This is my mother's avatar."

Yuchi's sword flew into a defensive position. "It is a breach of the user agreement to inhabit any avatar not registered to and linked with the user's account. You have openly admitted to this violation. As prescribed in the user agreement, your avatar will be immediately destroyed. Remain still as I—"

Laporte sprung, caging Yuchi in his grasp. The pair fell backward, each tumble and tuck on the stairs announced with a *clunk*.

Somehow, her guide still managed to speak through it like nothing abnormal was happening. "Third door on the right. Hurry, I'll deal with this."

At the second-floor landing, Laporte managed to knock the sword from Yuchi's hand.

"But—"

"Don't worry about me. I'm immortal here. You are not. Now, go."

Cindira raced forward, hoping that if it was true Laporte could take on any form he wanted, he really should transition to one with bigger muscles.

twenty-three

Cindira pulled back the sheer curtain, revealing a stained-glass window lit from behind, the image, a knight slaying a six-legged dragon. Only, instead of white-glazed panels to comprise the knight's face, was a void, a peephole where one could look out, the design hiding her features in plain sight.

Below, the typical scene of so many of the archaic animated films played out in faux flesh, bone, and blood. Gowns, suits, musicians donning powdered wigs and playing wooden instruments, chandeliers blazing with a hundred candles each, couples working their way through carefully rehearsed steps, servants (mostly male, and wearing dressed down styles of the wealthy and affluent users around them) with trays filled with the very food she'd seen being prepped not an hour before navigating the guests, a fountain shooting a chocolate stream into which several women were dipping bits of cake or fruit...

The fairy tale, just as marketed.

A glitch at the corner of her eye proceeded Laporte's reappearance, as though he were some sort of wizard popping into existence at will.

"Laporte! You scared me." Cindira leapt back, her hand flattening on her chest. "Yuchi?"

"Is rebooting. The process, combined with some road blocks I was able to throw up, will take about an hour."

It wasn't much time, but it would have to be enough. She turned back to the window, studying the crowd below, looking for Francisco's face, though she found it increasingly difficult to focus. So many luxuries and baubles on which the eye could catch. Curiosity burned within her: who were these people, and why were they here?

Despite the situation, Cindira's mouth crooked in delight. Awe was an understatement. She had coded individual artifacts, like Kaylie's intricate dresses, but the rich tapestry of the full view before her...how was it possible this was not *real*?

121

"You are impressed." It was a statement, not a question.

Cindira couldn't bring herself to lie, despite a little voice inside her reminding her that her mother never wanted this. "How could I not be? GAIA is amazing, but its buildings, its landscapes... Even the virtual weapons armies use to face each other in the Arenas of War... They're all direct reproductions of things that exist in the real world. But these things...the fashion, the style, the building...this hasn't existed for hundreds of years, but there it all *is*."

"Despite the old saying, Miss, I don't believe you only get one chance to make a *first* impression." Laporte pointed to the crowd below. "From up here, you see the big picture, the illusion of the cover story. Look *closer*. Look into the subtext of what really lies before you."

She need only to relax her gaze to see through the noise and take in the nuance as Laporte narrated the scene.

"That couple dancing there?" he said, pointing. "The prime minister and president of two countries currently warring inside GAIA, laughing and smiling as though they hadn't a care in the world. The lanky man standing at the fountain who'd just popped a strawberry in his mouth? A prime minister elected with questionable legitimacy, who just a few weeks ago had been indicted by the Gaian court of real world war crimes."

Laporte pivoted, this time indicating the far end of the ballroom where a woman who'd retreated to a mezzanine invisible to those below remained in plain sight of their current position. She grinned as a man accompanying her and dressed to the nines pushed her to the ground, lifted her skirt, and shoved his head into the folds of muslin, disappearing from view.

"Mira Labati, the famous actress currently on trial for killing her husband, and the journalist whose been assigned by *Tiempo Nuevo* to cover the case."

With eyes much sadder than any non-human's should be, Laporte gazed at Cindira. "Tybor promises the chance to relive a romantic past, but the past was never romantic. This world never existed. It still doesn't." Her companion shook his head. "Your mother dreamed of a world united, where disputes and conflict could be resolved in the interest of peace and prosperity, without destroying lands or lives. And then, Tybor held up a mirror to her vision, everything reflecting here, backward. Everything that GAIA is, this is the opposite. If your mother had lived, she would have done everything in her power to keep this from prospering. And your father..."

Suddenly, Cindira's heart raced. "What about him?"

His eyes dropped to the floor. "When you said you intended to come here, I thought I should stop you. You've placed yourself in tremendous harm just by logging in. But I also knew it was an opportunity for you to learn the truth."

"Laporte." Cindira turned from the window, forgetting the swirling plays of indulgence below. "Why are you bringing up my father?"

The mouse stepped away from the window and towards a wardrobe that sat on the edge of the room, a monstrously huge thing styled to look of mahogany and cherry wood. Inside, there were no blankets or linens or even dresses. There was an archway, and beyond that, another room.

With a hand gestured toward what lay beyond her field of vision, Laporte invited her to see past the fairy tale and discover the facts. "I'm afraid he may be a victim of it."

Everything about The Kingdom was impractical, but none of it until now had been impossible.

"Dad?"

What Cindira saw defied her understanding of the vreal world. Whenever a user was rendered unconscious, the avatar was *supposed* to return to the storage files. Yet, there was her father, laid out in a four-poster bed festooned with richly-embroidered green curtains and matching bed clothes. Or at least, there was her father's avatar.

"Dad? Dad!" Cindira shook her father's shoulder, gently at first, then harder. Try as she might, he would not wake.

The man beside her recalled his mouse behaviors when his head twitched, examining the sight before them. "The most recent entry recording your father's arrival to the palace grounds was two months ago, but I could find no logout record for him after that time."

"Two *months*?" Rage turned to worry. Cindira sat on his bed, stroking her father's stubble-strewn cheek. "You mean that my father's been lying here like this since February?"

"I cannot say. As you'll recall, I can only detect when someone passes a checkpoint into another section of the platform; I cannot tell where within that section they've been or are." Laporte circled the bed and sat on the opposite side. "His avatar is in stasis, much as your mother's was."

A crushing weight materialized in her stomach. "Are you saying my father is dead?"

Laporte shook his head. "No, not at all. There's still a flow of data in him between the real world and the vreal world, even if a minimal amount. Wherever it is he's jacked in from, it's a pirate signal, otherwise we could trace it and know where his body is. But, this I can tell you: he *is* alive."

The anxiety that had smoked her soul rose into the sky and dissipated. The bounce faded when her analytical mind raced to piece together what had happened. Two months was a long time to be missing without anyone noticing, but Cindira had noticed. When she went to Johanna, her step-mother always had an excuse. *"He's still in Asia." "There was need for him to stop in Istanbul." "An urgent request from one of our partners in Bangalore."* It seemed unlikely that Johanna would have been unaware of the truth, that Rex Tieg was black boxed inside The Kingdom.

The glitch was exceedingly rare, but it happened once or twice a year. Something would go wrong with a login or logout and the user's avatar and mind would end up somewhere in the abyss of code, unable to go one way or another. But that problem was one easily solved. Why hadn't Johanna solved it, then? PR? The implications of the CEO of the company being stuck?

Or was there a reason she didn't want this fixed? Or, if Cindira gave her step-mother the benefit of a doubt, that Johanna *couldn't* fix.

"If he isn't dead, is it possible that he's in a..."

Laporte, as if by magic, ceased to exist.

A different voice filled the void. "A coma?"

Cindira shot to her feet and even considered running, but it would do no good. Johanna was between her and the only door in or out of the room. Keeping her face to her father, her back to her step-mother, Cindira turned her head over her shoulder only enough to see the snake that had her cornered.

Johanna stepped with deliberate precision, the skirting of the very dress that Cindira herself had designed only the night before swaying like the head of a cobra. "You're not a servant bot, even though you're dressed like one. Who are you and how did you get in here?"

Cindira kept her face turned away from her step-mother, the cloth around her head shielding her face. "I'm…" *His daughter.* But she wasn't. At least, not when she was using her mother's avatar. "Someone concerned for his safety."

"You suppose I am not?" Venom laced Johanna's tone. "If you were so concerned for his safety, you wouldn't keep him like this. You'd free him."

What the hell? "You think *I* did this to him?"

"Do you suppose I did? Why would I put my own husband into a coma?"

"Because it gives you unchecked control of Tybor." Cindira labored to keep her tone flat, the timber of her mother's voice concealed. "I know who you are, Johanna Tieg. I know how you love power and influence and money—all of which you've been consolidating for years."

Johanna stopped at the foot of the bed, still one step behind so as not to see Cindira's face. She pointed to the mute avatar laying in the bed. "You mean, which *you've* been consolidating. And soon enough, when I find out how, I *will* crush you. Whoever you—"

The manicured fingernails bit into Cindira's shoulder. She cried out, even as Johanna spun her around. Cindira regained her footing only in time to look up and see her step-mother lose her own. The woman stumbled backward in shock.

"Impossible."

This programming? So robust. Johanna's skin blanched, her pupils dilated. Her step-mother threw a hand over her mouth, the

125

diaphanous material of the dress sleeve Cindira herself had designed, billowed.

"Omala?"

twenty-four

"There's still time to change your mind."

Francisco pulled back as the door to the kitchens swung closed. That there was a kitchen in The Kingdom surprised him. That was a change. No one ever ate food while logged into GAIA. Coffee remained a mainstay, though only because the habit was so ingrained in the real world, those transitioning to the virtual one for work found it difficult to go without. Even rendered as an avatar, psychological dependencies proved tough to defeat.

But as the prince came to terms with that fact, he remembered it was only one small part of the larger picture in this platform, one tailored for indulgences without consequences. Of course, there was food. More food in this one palace than in all the peasant kitchens of his homeland combined, likely. And as he looked out on the dance floor, he saw it was merely one excess this world boasted.

His trusted attaché, Carlos, waited as ever he did; tolerantly, silently, reverently. He had the patience of a saint and the combat skills of a warlord.

Francisco shook his head. "No. When I campaigned for office last year, I vowed to the Congress that ferreting out the corruption that goes on here would be my top priority."

"No one takes a campaign promise at face value, Your Highness."

"I do." He turned back, pushing the swinging door just enough to give himself a view of the ballroom beyond. "GAIA saved the world from destruction, Carlos, but that hit the bank accounts of many people in that room out there – at least one of whom is trying to destroy GAIA now. Most likely, more than one. They want me to cower, to stay hidden. I'm here to show them I'm not afraid."

"One might suggest you *should* fear them," Carlos cautioned. "They've penetrated GAIA's security, a system that has remained unhackable for a quarter century, not once but three times in as many weeks. There is no reason to think they'd be any less lethal in the real world. Pretending to be one of them may backfire in more ways than you've imagined."

"You forget, I *was* one of them. Living for the moment, letting my family's power, influence, and wealth be excuses I made for my own sense of entitlement..."

His thoughts turned back to his visit to Tybor, and playing into Kaylie Fife's flirtations, just to get to the truth he was seeking. His stomach had turned with every touch. In a few minutes, he'd repeat the process, and this time, backing out after getting to the answer of a simple yes or no question wouldn't be possible. He needed to seduce her, get her to trust him. Either she knew the truth of what was going on inside of GAIA, or she knew the people who did. *She associates with all the power brokers. She's slept with many of them.* In the virtual world, at least, his spies had told him. His analyst argued on whether or not she was simply the kind of woman who liked to boast of rendezvous with the famous and powerful, or if plots lay underneath her conquests. Francisco suspected the latter; she was the daughter of Johanna Tieg. A snake gave birth to snakes, and once he came to know her better, he suspected to find a serpent in his grasp.

A mirror mounted over a nearby sink let him check his hair with an informed eye. Later, he'd wonder at the washbasin's presence. Did this vreal world really have need of disinfectant? For now, he needed to be prepared. In a moment, he'd be walking openly among the enemy.

"I don't expect to find out who's behind the attacks on the capital tonight. If I make them believe I'm still one of them, I think it could lead to the anarchists outing themselves. *The secret lies in confusing the enemy, so that he cannot fathom your true intentions.*"

"Sun Tzu." Carlos allowed him an approving nod. "An appropriate tome to study for the times. But I believe he also said, *The wise warrior avoids battle.*"

"Yes, but wasn't it rumored that he, himself, *died* in battle?"

Francisco's attaché raised a scrupulous eyebrow. "If he ever truly existed at all."

"If any of us every truly exist at all." *Enough. No more stalling.* "Wish me luck, Carlos."

"Luck is for those who have no faith in liberty, Sire."

Francisco pushed the door open and observed in amazement as a room full of theatrics turned its spotlight on him. In the span of a moment, his courage fled back in time, and he saw himself as a youth, trembling on the stairs of his family's veranda, watching his father's blood trickle down each step. The people turned to him expectant, some perhaps ignoble. He could see it in their eyes: *So, this is the great prince without a kingdom who thinks he can challenge us?*

He wondered the same thing. His father's watch hung heavy on his wrist.

Francisco opened his mouth to speak, for they seemed to want him to say something. But what could he say? I *know one of you has been trying to kill me? I suspect one of you is trying to destroy GAIA?* It wasn't exactly diplomatic.

As he felt an arm weave through his and turned to see who was at his side, he thanked God for small miracles. Kaylee Fife: the in-girl of the in-crowd. The moment she appeared, the crowd relaxed. As though Francisco were a bomb and Kaylie had just snipped his tripwire.

"Your Majesty?" She hooked her arm around his. "I was beginning to worry you were going to skip out on the party, which would make you an intolerably bad host. Having cold feet about joining the soiree?"

Francisco plastered on his best public face, grinning as though the woman beside him had just said the most amazing thing. "Of course not, Miss Fife. I've been anticipating it all week."

She patted his arm and began to pull him toward the crowd. Kaylie leaned in, talking so only he could hear, even as the guests began to fall in to shake the prince's hand. "Just stay by my side. I'll make sure you only have to talk to the right people."

He bit his tongue, fighting back the truth he already knew.

There were no right people in this place.

And that included him.

twenty-five

Cindira's future balanced on a single decision: let Johanna believe her rival was indeed facing her down, admit to being Cindira, or keep both facts hidden.

She pulled herself erect, trying to embody her mother's mannerisms. "I'm not who you think I am."

Johanna threw back her head and cackled, balled fists planted on her hips. "Who you are is a fool. Don't you know that the moment I leave here, I will call Tybor's security and reveal who you are?"

"Then I'll make it easy for you. I'm the same person who hacked into GAIA a few days ago."

Johanna blanched, her eyes going wide. Despite the terror etched in her features, she let none of her anxiety creep into her voice. "I see."

Sending a shockwave over her step-mother empowered Cindira. Before she could pan out the pros and cons of assuming control, she was simply doing it. She pointed at the bed. "This avatar belongs to Rex Tieg. Why is he like this? What are his current whereabouts in the real world?"

"It's me who should ask you that. Instead, let me ask how you designed an avatar that looks and sounds exactly like Omala Grover? QC should have tagged that. Unless..." The blonde bit her lip in momentarily contemplation. "Was there one still hidden somewhere? One that's escaped my detection all these years?"

Cindira wouldn't be detoured. "What have you done to try and solve this?"

Johanna's head tilted to the side. "The very thing you told me to: I reached out to the prince. He's below right now, only he's not being as forthcoming as you suggested he would be. Don't worry, Kaylie will have him eating out of the palm of her hand soon enough, but I repeat: If you harm one hair on Kaylie or Cade's head, I will march down there and tell Batista everything I know."

Cindira didn't know what shook her more: her blatant dismissal by her step-mother, so ready to defend her own children with no reference to her, or knowing that the prince was now falling into one of Johanna's schemes.

The code writer was equally skilled in math and added up the figures pretty quickly. "You told Kaylie to seduce him."

"I'm going to have her *distract* him," Johanna amended. "If the prince finds out that our CEO is being held for ransom, do you think he'll overlook it? If the public knows, what do you think will happen to Tybor? Can I remind you that your ends, as hideous as they are, require my company to stay robust for now?"

"A human life isn't worth the cash flow of your hedonistic escape." Cindira balled her hands into fists as she took one more look at her father on the bed. "You've made a mockery of Omala Grover's legacy, and there will be consequences. *He* should not be one."

"There now, you've found your place in your standard script again." Her step-mother sat herself on the edge of the bed, stroking Rex's face. "I don't know how much you knew about Omala—the *real* Omala—but she wasn't exactly Rex's fan at the end, and she wasn't the squeaky-clean 'goddess' those crazy chipheads hold her out to be. In fact, she was actively trying to destroy The Kingdom *and* Tybor. Of course, that's what you and your cult want too, isn't it?"

Something about the way Johanna broke down before her, how her complete focus was on the man in the bed as she raised his hand to her mouth, kissed his palm, and then pressed it against her cheek, cracked Cindira's resolve. *Johanna may be a power-hungry, fame-seeking, money-grubbing nuisance, but the woman does love her husband.* And Rex? Despite the fact that he'd left Cindira's mother, turning his back on his child and the legacy they'd built together, one couldn't claim with any validity that he didn't feel the same for Johanna.

"I swear to you, I'm not part of whatever group it is you think I am." Cindira backed away from the bed. "Is he safe here like this?"

"His mind is, trapped between the real world and The Kingdom. Where his body is…" A tear streaked down Johanna's cheek as she looked up. "…I don't know what kind of condition he's in or what kind of care is being taken with him."

"Will you continue to protect him?"

131

"Always."

Cindira nodded, reaching for her resolve. She didn't have much time; Yuchi would be back online soon enough, and when she was, Cindira would be toast.

"I will find a way to help him."

Johanna's head jerked up. "How?"

"I..." Could she really do this? Expose her greatest truth? But she was safe, wasn't she? Johanna didn't know who she was, and if Yuchi's read was any indication, Tybor's security system saw her as Omala. "I'll dig into the source code. I can find a solution."

Her step-mother shot to her feet. "Impossible. No one but Omala Grover could access the source code."

All else being equal, the simplest solution was usually the correct one.

Even if it was a lie.

Cindira gathered her courage into a ball and shot it up her spine. "I *am* Omala Grover."

"No, you're not."

Commit to it. Sell it like you would a pretty gown. "You said it yourself, Johanna; only Omala could access the code, and I'm telling you, I'm here to do just that."

"I don't know who you are, but you're *not* Omala Grover."

Johanna's eyes narrowed as her hands came up before her. Only, they didn't look merely like hands. They looked like... flames. Blue flames that sparked and crackled and danced over her stepmother's arms. *Magic in The Kingdom*? Of course. It was a fairy tale, wasn't it? And real fairy tales didn't have happy endings and golden sunsets.

The Little Mermaid turned to sea foam.

Sleeping Beauty was assaulted and forced to wed her rapist.

The wolf ate Red Riding Hood's grandmother.

"I know you're not..." Johanna pulled back a hand, the energy

132

dancing over her skin coalescing into a ball on her open palm. "... because *I* killed her."

"No, that's not..."

Cindira froze, incapable of comprehension. It wasn't possible. Her mother's death had been a tragic accident. She'd fallen off a dock and been hit by the very boat coming to pick her up, her struggle covered over by the sound of the motor and the blanket of fog.

Cindira looked at the gown her step-mother wore, the one Cindira herself had made, invoking the somber purple drift of the fog itself. How ironically appropriate.

"And I'll kill her again, even if it's just her avatar!"

The flame shot forward, but shock immobilized Cindira. Her mother slain, her father in a coma, and Johanna the connection between each. She wanted to be done, to wake up in her own body and flee.

Moments before the flames scorched, a wall of white shot up between the women. Johanna's volley flattened, spread out as if it had been hurled into a shield.

"Run now, or you'll never save your father!"

She didn't know whose voice it was, or where it came from, but it snapped her out of her spell. Cindira bolted towards the door.

twenty-six

"And this..." Kaylie pulled on Francisco's arm, leading him to yet another elegantly-dressed couple, "Is Nugato Shoji and his wife, Kiki."

Instead of offering a hand, the gentleman bowed, a gesture somewhat archaic but still practiced in some areas of Asia. Not wanting to be insensitive, Francisco returned the gesture.

"Sir. Madame."

Another of the attendees begged away Kaylie's attention, leaving Francisco to fend for himself.

"So this is the brave Prince of GAIA." The woman passed judgement with both tone and a shaded eye. "They say your avatar is true to your real-world self. How disappointing."

"I think what Kiki is trying to say—" Nugato side-eyed his wife, who only rolled hers in turn. "—is that we're surprised you're brave enough to show your true face. So few in The Kingdom do."

"Something I believe should change," the prince said. "How can we negotiate terms of peace and trade in good faith if we cannot even take each other at face value? Though, I admit, I think minor cosmetic edits are okay." He pointed to his left ear. "There's actually a scar here in real life."

The couple on the receiving end of the jest didn't know what to make of it. They weren't the only ones. Francisco had no idea what to make of them, or the rest of the crowd. Sovereigns, dignitaries, celebrities... None of whom he could assign an obvious agenda in his imagination. And though many were indifferent or slightly disdainful of his presence, none appeared outwardly aggressive.

But the slightest scent of possible scandal filled the air, and the nearest shark bit. Suddenly, Kiki found Francisco a lot more interesting.

"A scar?" She leaned in closer, as though she could see it if she only squinted hard enough. "How exciting. From what?"

134

"When I was fourteen, assassins broke into my family's home and killed my father in front of my eyes. I tried to fight them off but one smashed his gun on my forehead to knock me out. I woke up with blood in my eyes and my father's corpse staring at me from the stairs."

Francisco sipped his wine, even as Kiki scrambled for something to say.

She was saved by her husband weaving his arm through hers and saying, "Our sympathies for your loss," before leading her away.

Francisco wished he could say their attitude was unique, but he knew better. Even though he hadn't spent his youth gallivanting around The Kingdom, a diplomatic bit of eavesdropping would educate anyone ignorant of its ways. Francisco had mastered the art of looking forward, leaning left. He could follow two conversations at once when he concentrated, even if briefly.

Those around the fringes didn't hesitate to engage in their standard business. An illegal trade deal was the least of the sins his ears tripped over. To his right, two men discussed the details of deep earth mineral extraction, a process that would ravage the lands above it. GAIA had outlawed the practice in the second year of its existence.

Then, an accented male voice rose up behind him, and it made him want to jack out that very second.

The prince rounded, his eyes scanning the crowd for his heretofore undesired escort. Now he'd give his castle for Kaylie to be at his side, if only to use her as a human shield.

"Well, well, if it isn't His Majesty, *Prince* Francisco Batista de le Reina."

The words arrested him as well as if he'd been bound and shackled. The man at his back may as well have been a herald shouting at the top of his lungs. Francisco was certain the invocation reverberated off the walls. At the very least, his pulse was.

With no choice but to confront his past head on, he found his spine and put it to good use.

Francisco turned, pushing a hand out and a smile on to his face all at once. The confidence might be conjured, but diplomacy called for a skill. "Hugo Ferrente Miguel."

He'd expected to see the wizened, battle-scarred face of his lifelong adversary, framed in graying, spiked hair and with one eye bandaged over, lost in one of the last real-world skirmishes to take place on the Iberian Peninsula before the region dedicated itself to the GAIA platform. Instead, a younger iteration of his former friend, skin as perfect and unblemished as it been when they were youths.

Hugo's smile fell, as his grip on Francisco's hand tightened. "You forgot to say *King*."

To acknowledge his intention would be to prove the insult. Instead, Francisco changed subject. "I didn't imagine you'd still be patronizing this place after so many years."

"Fifteen years isn't so very long." Hugo took back his hand. "Especially when there are estates and family to care for, it keeps one very busy."

The arrow hit its mark. Francisco hoped no one else noticed his half-step retreat. Except for El Castillo Circulo, nothing remained of his ancestral estate. And family? Hugo's army claimed his only uncle, and despair in the wake of so much loss, his mother.

Then, to add insult to injury, Hugo had stolen Francisco's first love.

Hugo continued. "I have to admit, I was surprised to learn you'd put yourself up for election. I was astonished even more when you won."

"Yes, well, GAIA was founded primarily for the benefit of the poor and powerless, both of which your betrayal left me."

"Oh, come now, Francisco. Surely you must have had a little *something* put away. Don't tell me you were able to seize one of the most powerful offices in the world through a demonstration of leadership, especially when you've never shown that particular skill as far as I'm aware."

Rage made Francisco's fists curl, but experience kept his tongue still.

Hugo seemed disappointed. "No response to that? Maybe you have learned something then. But tell you something…" Flexing his index finger, Hugo invited Francisco to lean in. "You can keep up this every-man charade for a while, but eventually, they're all going

136

to figure out who you really are. I only hope you come to terms with it before they do."

Pulling back, Hugo offered his hand again. "It was good to catch up, Francisco."

But the prince was through playing politics. He turned away, fuming, clutching the place that he wore his father's watch in the real world. He needed to be reminded of what he was fighting against, the kind of hedonistic crime that still went on, despite GAIA's existence.

He needed to make sure that Omala Grover – and his own father – hadn't died in vain.

twenty-seven

Her step-mother's ball gown was fabulous, a tribute to indulgence and wealth. It had no less than ten petticoats, and underneath, a proper corset.

And it was one hell of a burden to move in.

Cindira turned a corner and found another hall, this one with four doors. Three were locked, but the fourth mercifully opened. A set of service stairs took her down to a hall lit by candles, and with only one exit. Cindira ran the length of the hall and opened the door.

And immediately slammed it shut.

Somehow, she'd come to the edge of the ballroom.

That the other servants were bots was obvious to Cindira the moment she looked in. Sure, those servicing the buffet, removing dishes, or refilling wine glasses appeared human on first glance, but they shared a certain sameness noticeable with just a little examination.

A sameness, sadly, that Cindira did not share. Firstly, because she was a she, and none of the others in the ballroom were. Second, because while she had the same bhindi the VAPORSs did, it was different somehow. It didn't...

It didn't glimmer! Had that been why the diodes she sometimes integrated into Kaylie's designs were contraband? If anyone else noticed, her gambit ended then and there.

If only she could quit the program and wake up back in the world, she would, but Cindira realized with a lurch in the base of her stomach that she had no clue how to get out of the program.

How had she gotten out of GAIA?

Oh, yeah, that's right. An explosion.

That didn't seem very doable, did it?

"Go into the ballroom!"

Cindira squealed as something small and furry crawled over her foot. "Laporte?"

He was a mouse again, which was just as well. He certainly was more portable that way, and if there was one thing she needed, it was to keep moving.

"Sorry I disappeared," he said as she picked him up. "Johanna doesn't know about me, and it's best if that remains the case."

Even though he wasn't real, even though he was just the manifestation of codes, algorithms, and AI, he was the closest thing to a confidante she had. Maybe that was why she found herself confessing to him. "She killed my mother."

The mouse blinked. "What?"

"Johanna killed my mother," Cindira said. "She just told me. She just... Oh, my god. All this time, for years, and I...my father is..."

"Miss, I hate to sound uncaring. We *will* use this knowledge, but for now, you are here. If you're to do something, it must be now," Laporte, balancing on her shoulder, advised. "Time is running out."

Her heart pounded, but why should she panic? It was just another puzzle to solve, another task to complete. Or so she tried to tell herself. "Won't the midnight protocol kick me out before then?"

"Not before Yuchi revives. Your mother's avatar cannot be destroyed, but your tether to it *can* be severed. We cannot allow that to happen. We'll get you to an exit, but the closest public portal is outside the palace gates. If Yuchi kicks it off the platform, Omala's avatar will merely reiterate back in the magic pumpkin. You, however, will not."

"Oh, my god." Cindira stopped in her tracks. "This is my mother's *actual* avatar from our apartment, isn't it?"

"That's not important right now. We have twenty minutes until Yuchi recovers, and we must get you out before then."

Why was that important? "Didn't you hear what I said? My mother is dead, and Johanna killed her."

"And will you just sit here and allow her to do the same to you?"

139

"Of course not. But how could she? You can't die in the—"

Laporte cut her off. "The Kingdom isn't like GAIA. Here, if you die in the program, you die in the real world."

Her blood became ice. "But that's against every international law written. It's murder!"

"It's the least of Tybor's offenses."

She shook her head, trying to fit in this revelation with the company ran by her father. "How often does that—"

"Don't think about it now. I can tell you the details later. For now, focus. Find the prince. Do what you came here to do. You're unlikely to have another chance like this."

But the wheels in Cindira's mind refused to halt. The implications of such a policy sprinted down a tree of logic, leaving to one, single inevitable conclusion.

So that was why Johanna had agreed to let Francisco host this ball.

Cindira was up and moving into the ballroom before Laporte could even complete the sentence. "Oh my god, the prince!"

twenty-eight

Cindira surveyed the room. Francisco was easy enough to find, all she need do was follow everyone's eyes. Kaylie had become a barnacle on the side of the ship of state. They weren't that far away. Ten, fifteen feet? With their backs to the tables covered in food, Kaylie and Francisco's position wasn't exactly unbreachable. Cindira could probably shout his name and he'd hear. If they weren't in a room surrounded by potential enemies, she may do just that.

"I have to get him out of here. The explosion in GAIA...if someone tries that here, he won't survive. And why wouldn't they try?"

Cindira looked back over her shoulder just in time to see a swish of purple petticoats round the door that she'd come through moments before. Given the fact that her step-mother's hands no longer flamed and burned, she was willing to bet the whole magic thing wasn't exactly widely known. Of course, it wasn't. If the others became aware such a thing was possible, they'd be knocking down Tybor's doors for the upgrade.

"Laporte, how much time is there between Yuchi coming back online and the stroke of midnight protocol activates?"

"Five minutes, ten seconds."

Five minutes of vulnerability? She'd have to make it work.

"Can you summon that coach to the front steps?"

The mouse chirped. "I'll have to drive it myself, but yes. I'll need a minute, Miss, then I'll be outside. Just there, at the far end of the room."

She turned, seeing a set of open double doors beyond which the light of the ballroom danced over cobblestones and a fountain. Even from the occluded rear view, Cindira recognized the ceremonial entrance at the front of the Palace from Tybor's marketing materials.

"Don't be late," she told the mouse.

141

Laporte scurried off her shoulder, down her skirting, and deftly wove between hundreds of feet to the front entrance.

Cindira needed to both get out and get the prince out. Should she walk right up and talk to him? A servant being so bold would run against programming, immediately mark her as a fraud.

Catch his eye and hope he'd make his way to her? No good; he'd drag every eye in the room with him.

Damn it! She needed to extricate him, and do so in a way where he couldn't just immediately dismiss her or run away completely.

From her right, a servant bot approached, in his hands a tray on which sat a steaming, succulent leg of lamb and a very, very sharp knife.

Everything here is a weapon, if you figure out a way to use it.

But in the Stadium, weapons aren't fatal. In here, they are. This might as well be real life.

She had the blade in hand and pressed to Francisco's throat before she could give the plan, or the idea that this was *real*, too much thought.

The prince managed nonchalance and threw his hands up in the air. "I don't know who you are, but I will. Everyone will. Let me go now, and you stand a chance at surviving this."

The crowd pulled back, as though they were the ones under threat. All except Kaylie, who planted her balled up fists on her hips (as well as could be done, given the corset she wore beneath her gown to hold it in the right shape), and took two steps forward.

Didn't they know who she was? The Gaian prince didn't recognize Omala Grover's voice? Only then did Cindira realize that standing behind a man three inches taller effectively hid her from the crowd. All they could really see were her eyes, her arm, and the hand holding the blade.

He spoke softly, as though he didn't want the others to overhear. "What is it you're hoping to get away with? Slit my throat, it will—"

"Quiet!" She backstepped, leading them along the edge of

the buffet table, towards the doors that led outside. There wasn't time to explain to him. If she didn't get him out of here and warn him of the true danger he was in before the midnight protocols swept her out, he'd really be in trouble. "Just… stay quiet and keep walking backwards."

He complied, all while chuckling lowly. "I never thought I'd be the kind of person to say this, but…do you know who I am?"

Francisco yelped as Cindira's arm jerked him back a little harder. "Do you think I'd be doing this if I didn't?"

"Then you must know there's no way you're going to get away with this."

"You should pray I do, or you're never going to survive tonight."

The moment they were outside, the whiny of horses and rambling of wheels came into the foreground. Back in his human incarnation, Laporte perched on the driver's seat of the coach. The door opened without her undertaking the effort. More magic, or an automated sequence written in the code for convenience despite the intended aesthetic? She'd have to wonder about that later.

The crowd funneled outside as Cindira lowered the knife, spun the prince, and used the blade to indicate the intended action. To his credit, he didn't seem the slightest bit intimated. His cool compliance in itself, an act of bravery. Of course, he didn't understand the true threat, so why would he worry? His avatar had been murdered before, and he'd woken up back in his own body in the real world.

Just as Cindira got a foothold to step into the coach, Johanna muscled her way to the front of the crowd.

"Mark my words, you've overplayed your hand," she shouted.

Cindira pondered the years that passed since her mother's murder, swirled them with the moments since finding her father, and suddenly understood her place in the world.

"Don't you get it? I just opened a new deck of cards. And this? This is only the beginning."

Laporte pulled the reins, and they were off.

twenty-nine

Francisco was not scared.

He was livid.

And mystified.

And still, livid.

The woman collapsed back against the cushioned bench opposite him like the hard part was over. As the coach fled, she worked the coif over her head with her free hand, letting it fall to the seat beside her, and Francisco got his first unobstructed view of his kidnapper. Her voice had been familiar, but now with her long, black locks framing a face distinguished by high cheekbones, a nose that hooked slightly at the end, and brilliantly sand-hued skin, there could be no doubt.

Two possibilities to explain the impossible: either the woman before him was an impostor, or Omala Grover wasn't dead after all.

Her reverie blew away in seconds, and the woman's body jerked straight, as though a siren awoke her from a deep sleep. Until he was sure which possibility was true, Francisco had no intention of admitting he recognized the avatar before him. Or at least, its namesake.

She looked him in the eye. "The important thing to know is that I have no intention of hurting you."

"Intention only means you haven't conceived of hurting me, not that you've ruled it out completely." Francisco pointed to the knife she held out, though her grip had eased somewhat. "You might as well stab me and get all the angst out of your system. I'll wake up back in the real world, where I promptly contact Tybor and have your profile tracked, your jackpod's location revealed, and your ass, arrested."

"I think you'd find that easier said than done." She threw the knife on the seat *next to him*. "Here. If it makes you feel better, you hold it. I only threatened you with it to save you."

144

He snatched up the weapon while gazing at her with utter incredulity. "In what world do you save someone by putting a knife to their throat?"

"One where the knife is the lesser threat."

Even as the rocking coach sped out of the palace compound, the woman seemed uncertain of how to proceed. She hadn't expected this whole kidnapping thing to work, he theorized, and now that it had, she wasn't sure what to do next. Her chest heaved as she clutched at her hair, and he recognized the mannerisms as ones he himself had displayed whenever stretching his mental capabilities. Finally, she exhaled through funneled lips.

"Someone's trying to kill you."

"You mean besides you?" He feigned shock. "Do tell."

"I don't know much more than that.".

Francisco sat back, his eyes focusing on the scenery whisking by outside. "Well, isn't that convenient."

Suddenly, the coach slowed to a stop. Two ticks later, the driver, a diminutive young man looking vaguely Southeast Asian but attired in clothes befitting The Kingdom's baroque European aesthetic, opened the door. He nodded once to Francisco, then turned on the woman across the way.

"Miss, Yuchi went active four minutes ago and is presumably tracking us. I have just registered her passing out of the Palace zone. Best make use of the time left before the midnight protocol."

She nodded, then turned again on the prince. "Tybor doesn't have access to the source code. They've been trying for years to get into it, but my... *Omala Grover* put up the programming equivalent of a forest of thorns around it. There's only one living soul who can help you get to it, but she has to know what your intentions are."

Francisco kept all emotions from his face as he channeled his inner diplomat, even though what he really wanted was to take the knife to *her* throat and get her to talk. "Those are classified. But answer me this: why would Tybor's ability to access the source code be a bad thing?"

"Because then, they'd be unstoppable. This place—" She took

on a mocking air. "—this *Kingdom*—is where the enemies of GAIA are amassing, Your Highness, the people whose pockets grew fat from the type of conflict and horror GAIA's been solving for the last two decades. Destroying it would have consequences I can't accept, but I'll do what I can to help keep it contained."

"Why do you think I'm here? I'm not just a pretty figurehead. I'm the sovereign of the virtual world, and a strong influence on the real one. I'm aware of what The Kingdom really is, and the kind of power-hungry usurpers who frequent it."

He let pass the fact that once, he'd been one of them.

The woman nodded curtly. "Be that as it may, they want you dead. You were a fool to come here. Don't do it again. I'm not sure if I can get in again to help you, and frankly, I have more important people to save if I can come back."

The mousy man cried out again. "The time, Miss."

Not-Omala ignored him. "You have to understand, here isn't like GAIA. You die in The Kingdom, you die in the real world." Having dropped that bomb, her message must have been complete. The black-haired woman stood and exited the coach. "I have to go."

"Wait... What?" Francisco hopped out of the coach and gave chase, still clutching the blade she'd surrendered. She was already five feet away, moving as quickly as she could, almost as though she were being hunted. "If that's true, then why give me this—" he held up the knife. "—your only defense? I might have just stuck you with it, thinking all it would do would be to send you out of the program."

She paused and turned back. A smile lifted the corners of her mouth. "Because the kind of man whose instinct it is to save a child from an explosion—even a child he was convinced was an enemy—when he knows neither of them was really in danger, wouldn't stab a defenseless woman, even virtually."

Save a child from an explosion?

"It was you." Francisco's mouth had gone suddenly dry. "Omala? Are you still alive?"

"No, Omala's dead, no matter how much either of us wish otherwise."

146

"But the source code." *Who else would possibly know how?* "Please, GAIA needs your help. Don't…"

Footfalls rampaged, an angry figure cloaked in black armor and brandishing a sword ran towards them. A samurai? Here? It made no sense. He had no time to dwell on that, however, as the first clang of the bell descended from the clock tower over the palace gates, bringing with it an electrifying chill.

Goooonggg.

Francisco checked the facsimile of his Papa's watch. Midnight.

Not-Omala lashed her head around, her face paling. "Laporte?"

The petite man said, "She'll need to maintain a logistical framework to attack. It will be a disadvantage."

Francisco didn't understand who the samurai was, or why Not-Omala needed to run from her, but he did know the Asian woman across the way had one hell of a sword in her hand, and it made the knife the kidnapper had used look like a spatula. Before he stopped to think otherwise, Francisco threaded his hand through Not-Omala's, and pulled her with all his might. "We have to run!"

Goooonggg.

Their feet pounded, but their pursuer made a mockery of their flight. Lithe steps and swift feet weren't winning; the samurai ate the space between them with each step. It didn't help that whatever shoes Not-Omala had on clanked and clicked with each pump of her legs. All the while, that infernal clock tower rang from afar, reminding them that danger was coming at them from all levels.

Goooonggg.

Not-Omala stopped suddenly, yanking Francisco back and holding out her hand. "Quick, give me the knife!"

Was she crazy? "No, we can make it to the exit!"

She took the blade, despite his protest. "I need to make sure *you're* safe. You're the prince; I'm no one!"

Goooonggg.

"I *need* to get into the source code, before GAIA comes crashing down. If the person you know can help me do that—"

His argument seemed to win her over. Suddenly, her feet began to move.

Goooonggg.

They reached the port. A silver button on the frame of the door pulsed light, one of the few things to behave in a non-era conforming way in the platform. Francisco's hand smashed down, and inside his head, an internal countdown clock began to tick off the five-second delay required before jumping.

Five… Four….

Three… Two…

"No!"

Just as his foot fell forward, her hand left his.

Francisco spun and found disaster: the samurai, her left arm braced around not-Omala's neck, with the sword pushed against the base of his kidnapper's throat. A drop of blood trickled down from where the blade nicked her.

The samurai's speech held no accent. "Back away from the gate, Your Majesty."

Goooonggg.

Not-Omala's hands clutched around her captor's arm, but proved powerless to free herself, Not-Omala's lip quivered. "Don't listen to her. Go!"

His head swiveled between the situation before him and the exit behind him. "But she'll kill you."

"Think! I'm out at midnight, but why would she want you to stay?"

Goooonggg.

He'd been so wrapped up in the danger before him, he'd failed to anticipate that to come. Not-Omala made a good point: He was not only a free citizen, but the Prince of GAIA. What reason would this —she must be a security bot of some kind?— have for forcing his presence at such dire stakes if not for an ulterior motive?

And who was the woman held captive, that the samurai didn't just slay her on sight?

Someone who was of value to his enemies as well.

Someone... who knew how to access the source code.

Goooonggg.

Francisco looked upon the woman with newfound reverence. "It's you."

"Your Majesty—" The samurai's blade bit deeper, bringing a trickle chasing the path of the previous single drop. It must have hurt, but Not-Omala did nothing more than suck in a breath. "I must insist."

What could he do? *What could he do?* He couldn't let this woman die, and he couldn't succumb to threats.

But before he could act on his own, before he could even *decide* what to do, his options were taken away from him.

Not-Omala groaned, throwing all her weight back. The heel of her translucent shoe sped his direction. Instinct drove Francisco. Sensing an attack, he tried to catch her blow before it connected. All he managed was to get a hold of one of her curious slippers, which came off in his hands as the force of the maneuver threw him off balance and falling backward.

A moment was all it took for the samurai's sword to fall between them, slicing into Francisco's wrist just as his body passed through the portal.

Red everywhere.

Blood in his eyes.

Dead eyes staring into his soul.

"Breathe, Your Majesty! Breathe!"

His eyelids shot up, but the sight didn't bring clarity. All around him, GAIA security forces swarmed. He was still in his jackpod, but the lid had been lifted away. A pressure on his wrist forced him to pull his arm up to examine it, out of a physician's hands.

"Your Majesty! Wait." The woman yanked his arm back under his control. "I have to finish the wrapping. We'll get you to a medical suite as soon as we staunch the bleeding. Try to stay calm."

"Bleeding? I—"

His words tapered off where his confusion took over.

The physician looked up just long enough to grimace. "You have a deep cut to your right arm. It will require sutures."

"How? I was jacked in. How did I get injured while I was—"

But then it all came rushing back to him: the ball, the confrontation with Hugo, the kidnapping, the samurai.

The woman.

Francisco's head lashed to the side, finding two members of his tech team hovering on the periphery of the bubble about him. "The woman who abducted me. Who was she?"

They looked at each other in confusion. "Abduction?"

Of course, they wouldn't know. Anyone else at the ball would have had to leave the palace to exit as well. No chance Carlos had yet gotten back to reveal the emergency within, and his security officers only had tangential access to Tybor's system to observe.

No matter. Soon enough, the whole world would know.

Francisco yanked back his hand, pulling the damaged arm into his chest, and sat up, despite his physician's protestations.

"Find her!" He shouted. "I don't care what it takes, just find her!"

thirty

Goooonggg.

Any relief Cindira felt at seeing Francisco's form fall into a darkened doorway and, presumably, out of the platform evaporated when the tip of Yuchi's sword pierced her skin.

"Laporte?" Cindira's eyes moved in the direction of the fidgeting figure to the right. "What do I do?"

"I've determined the best option is to fight your way out."

The involuntary guffaw that erupted from her chest would have been funny any other time. "Seriously? Why can't you just do whatever you did back in the castle and force her to restart?"

Goooonggg.

"Because she's adapted to my attack; it wouldn't work a second time." Laporte came to her aid, pulling Cindira to her feet.

"Enough of your chattering!" Yuchi's hand flew out. If the dagger had been on her person somewhere, or if she'd conjured it out of air on a whim, Cindira couldn't say. Laporte's eyes bugged. He let out one very terrified shriek as he dissolved into a mouse and scurried away to safety underneath a nearby water trough.

"Laporte!"

Goooonggg.

Her shouting achieved nothing. It was too late.

As the resonance of the last bell dissipated, Cindira closed her eyes and accepted the inevitable. She would be booted out of The Kingdom. Would it kill her? Would it hurt? Would it somehow reveal her true identity? All these answers lay on the other side of midnight.

Only, nothing happened. She was still jacked in. She cracked open her eyes and looked down at her legs pressed into the ground before her. She no longer wore the servant attire. Her hands pressed to her face, recognizing not her mother, but her own.

With no one else to ask, Cindira looked up at the travel bot. "Why am I still here? How?"

Yuchi still held out her sword. "You are to wait."

"Wait?" Cindira scooted back, only for Yuchi to advance in her retreat. "For what?"

"An override to your rejection was ordered by the Queen. You will be detained until she arrives." At last, her weapon dropped to her side. "You will not be harmed as long as you are compliant."

The scenario played out in Cindira's mind in the snap of a second: Johanna's arrival, being discovered for who she really was, her step-mother's realization that she had confessed to Omala's own daughter the murder she'd committed. The possibility that a magic-wielding, world-controlling Johanna may decide it would be easier to kill Cindira here and cover up yet another death.

No, she couldn't let that happen. She must live. She must avenge her mother. She must save her father. She must protect GAIA.

"You're wrong about that, Yuchi." Cindira kneeled down, feeling the stem of the knife press into her hand. "I've been compliant all my life, and the only thing it's done is bring me harm."

Eyes shifting, grin lifting, the bot followed Cindira's movement like a cat sizing it's prey. "You don't really think you can take me, can you?"

"I can't defeat you, but I don't *need* to. The only thing I need to do is get through that portal."

The Kingdom wasn't reality. The vreal world was a creation of a genius but human mind, and AI or no, a human mind could rule it, change it, command it. Johanna had done it, tossing around waves of "magic," but magic wasn't real. *She's doing here what I do in the Stadium,* Cindira thought. *And if she can do that without knowing what I know, what couldn't I do if I tried?*

Her right arm lashed out, while her mind strung together the code to render what she'd imagined. Yuchi took a step back when the steak knife disappeared, and a rapier replaced it.

"You... You recoded it. While inside the platform! Impossible!"

152

Cindira kept her focus, lifting the sword back, to the right, to the ready. "We don't have to do this. Just let me leave."

The samurai mirrored the pose. "I cannot permit it."

Confusion. Noise. Strength. Fear. The swing of the katana brought them all in Cindira's direction.

She leapt back. Once. Twice. Volley. Block. Thrust.

Cindira fought with the might of the woman she was, and the child she'd been. Every attack was met in kind. Every strike, blocked. Every parry, met with equal rebuttal. Being able to conjure a sword out of nothing *was* impressive, but it was not indominable. Yuchi settled both her hands on her sword, rounding with a barbarous yelp in a spinning blow.

"Stand down!" Yuchi bellowed. "I will not harm you unless driven to do so."

Unless driven to do so...

Laporte's words echoed in her mind. *"She'll need to maintain a logistical framework to attack. It will be a disadvantage."*

If that was true, that meant Yuchi was subject to the same rules Cindira was. But whereas Yuchi was a creature born of code, who could only carry out programming and act on protocol, Cindira was not.

The katana fell away as the earth below the samurai's feet bubbled and stewed. A few lines of the program altered, inserted by Cindira's thoughts into The Kingdom's programming as a limited application. She'd made a sandbox of the place where Yuchi stood, and filled it with quicksand.

Cindira wasted no time. Jumping to her feet, she realized suddenly why her balance felt so uneven. One of her shoes was missing. Only, where was it?

The clop-clop of horse hooves filtered through the air, and she knew she'd have to leave it behind. It was only a vreal world manifestation of the glass slipper, after all. Surely its absence didn't imply anything more.

Eyes on the gate, Cindira dropped the sword in her hand, and threw herself forward, into to the exit portal.

thirty-one

Johanna stewed in her office, her eyes cataloguing the skyline that stretched out from their perch on Twin Peaks, down to where parts of the old city had been reclaimed by the tides. Across the Bay, Oakland twinkled, almost as if Omala, rotting in her grave, managed to laugh at her.

A knock on her door broke her reverie.

"Yes?"

Her assistant, Willa, had previously been Rex's for the last six years. She'd stopped asking when her boss would be coming back a week ago. Soon, she'd get suspicious that the story Johanna presented over and over was just that: a fairy tale.

Willa peeked around the corner. "Your daughter is here to see you, Mrs. Tieg."

"Tell Kaylie I'll come by her office in a little while."

Willa took two steps into the office. "Not *that* daughter."

"I only have one—"

Johanna cut herself off the moment she realized what the assistant meant. She sent the comque moments before, a request to Cindira to meet and discuss heightened security protocols. Covering up what had happened two nights ago in The Kingdom proved impossible; there were far too many witnesses. Damage control took priority now, should have taken priority from the start.

Cindira was the best coder Tybor had. The best coder anywhere, perhaps. For Tybor to survive this, Omala Grover's meek little step-daughter had a lot of work before her.

"Cindira? Already?"

Willa confirmed it with a nod. "Did you want me to send her away?"

"No, I—" Johanna smoothed out her jacket and cleared her

throat. "Show her in."

Johanna couldn't remember when she'd started hating her step-daughter. No matter what anyone claimed, it had not been since their first meeting. In fact, Johanna had been rather taken by the beautiful, precocious, and vastly intelligent eight-year-old child. So much so, that she envied Omala for her fortune.

But no matter how hard Johanna tried to win Cindira's heart, it was not to be done. Oh, the girl had never been disrespectful. On the contrary, Rex's child from his first marriage was gracious to a fault. After a while, that wore on Johanna. And, oh, how Rex doted on her. Who was this child to treat her cordially and distantly at the same time?

No, hate had not come first. First it was confusion, then bitterness. And then, jealousy. Jealousy when Johanna understood that Rex would always love his daughter so much more than he loved her, and that this daughter was so much like her mother that...

Well, when put that way, it seemed silly, but such was the human heart. Omala's death had been the perfect opportunity, it turned out, to exorcise Cindira from their lives. "Everything here will remind her of her mother," she'd told Rex. "She'll constantly be brought down by reminders at every turn. And she's so intelligent. Kaylie and Cade? They tease and taunt, and she doesn't deserve that. Boarding school is really the best thing for her now."'

Rex bought into the "mother's insight" line. *Such a fool.*

A fool she hadn't planned on loving but managed it anyhow.

"Surely you've heard about what happened." Tybor's commander kept her eyes turned to the city outside the windows as her step-daughter crossed the distance between the door and the chair in front of the desk with tentative, measured steps.

Cindira's tiny, unsure voice answered, "The prince, kidnapped. They say he's okay though. I read that some mysterious woman managed to hack her way into the program."

Johanna turned her gaze to the meek little coder. "We don't know if it was a woman." Johanna had suspicions, but none she planned to share in current company. "The avatar used belonged to a woman, but it, too, was hijacked. We should assume nothing."

The girl's eyes raced to the floor. "Of course." Then, barely looking up, she added. "How do you know the avatar was hijacked?"

"Because who it belonged to...there's no way that person could really be there. It's impossible."

Luckily, Cindira pressed no further, only nodding and looking back to her feet.

Johanna turned her attention back to the matter at hand. "So far, most of the press has accepted my explanation: the whole thing was a test to see if our security measures were as effective as we claimed them to be. They failed, and one rogue hacker was able to take advantage of the situation." Johanna leaned forward, her voice lowering. "But you and I know that's not what really happened, don't we?"

The young thing flushed. She never could take an authoritative tone well. "We do?"

"Yes, we do. Your mother was a genius. What, does it surprise you to hear me say that? You think I didn't respect her talents? She was a luminary, and you were her little doppelganger from the very first time I met you."

Cindira stayed maddeningly quiet.

Johanna smashed her palm against the desk. "Enough is enough, already. Admit you know how to access the source code, and then *do it*. Genius or no, we need to tap into the root directories and fortify The Kingdom, or it's all going to fall apart."

"But I keep telling you, I don't know how to get *into* the source code."

"Find a way. Clean up this mess made by the gaps in your mother's code! If you don't—"

It would sound like a threat, and for once, Johanna didn't want that. But what else could she say? It was the truth.

"If you don't," the blonde's chest fell as she exhaled, "then you're probably going to be an orphan very soon."

Cindira looked like a caught fish trying to understand how she'd ended up on land. "I'm sorry?"

Now that the can of worms was open, nothing remained but to bait the hook. "Your father isn't traveling. He's been kidnapped. *Kidnapped*, sound familiar? The same tactic used by the hacker who broke into The Kingdom. I don't doubt they are one in the same."

For a girl who harped on about the inability to reach her father for months, Cindira took the news with amazing poise. "Is that so?"

Perhaps the estrangement between daughter and father she'd long sought had come to pass unnoticed.

"It is," Johanna continued. "His avatar is laying in stasis in The Kingdom, under my care. I can't track the connection, can't break him free. For two months now, Cindira. Even in the best of circumstances, how much longer can I expect his real-world body to endure?"

"But why would someone kidnap my father? For money?"

"If they wanted money, they would have made demands by now. What they want is power. What they want...is the source code."

There was the reaction she'd been looking for: shock, confusion, disappointment, fear.

Especially fear.

"But anyone who has the source code for The Kingdom has the source code for GAIA. They could destroy everything my mother built, and in the process, release war back into the real world."

"If we want to save your father, what choice do we have?"

"It's not a choice," Cindira argued. "They want something we can't give them."

"They want something we can't give them *yet*." Johanna settled into her seat, and into her decision to press forward. "You are the single most talented code writer of your generation, and your skills don't stop there. Rumor has it that you show up in the hackdomes, and that you are undefeated."

The girl's eyes went to the floor as she shook her head. "I'm not sure I know what you mean."

"Like hell you don't. *Cade* saw you there a few weeks ago. For that offense alone, I could fire you, but I also know you're the best hope we have to save your father. You don't care about me, and we both know how I feel about you, but what about him? Won't you finally admit you know the code for *him*?"

Cindira kept her silence, but the guilt weighing down her features only emboldened Johanna.

"You have the skills. Use them!" she drove on. "Break into the source code. We can clean up the damage once he's safe."

"But what you're asking me to do is basically dismantle my mother's legacy."

"To save the life of the man we both love!" Johanna labored to tone down her rising voice. "You do love your father, don't you? You even changed your name after your mother died as a present to him."

Now she flashed red. "Of course, I love my father." And behind her eyes, Johanna read the unspoken allegation, *far more than you do*.

"Then help me. Draw out the people who've done this, and once they've crawled out of the shadows, we'll cut them down, once and for all."

thirty-two

Laporte wished he had the ability to listen in to the real world the way he could the virtual one. He could tunnel through tech, become a bug that wormed its way right into any other system around, but analysis suggested detection too likely. The events of two nights before had forced every security specialist Tybor had to report for duty. There were so many new tripwires being laid down in the code, even a mouse would have trouble not stumbling over them.

The door flew open, followed by a blur of blue cotton and black hair. Cindira didn't stop to speak. She went straight to the bathroom of the small pool house she and Asla shared and slammed the door behind her. A moment later came the sounds of retching.

Laporte's patience could rival a mountain's most days, but he found himself...curious. He tried to tell himself it was a result of programming, that it was merely the intersection of new knowledge and his lack of it. But there was something more there. *Concern*? That was a human emotion. Machines were meant to be impartial. His programming gave him a mission, not the other way around.

Finally, after several minutes, his master reemerged, pale as a sheet and with strands of hair stuck to her face.

"Miss?"

She held up a hand as she struggled to the couch, collapsing the moment she arrived. "I'm *stronger* now. I'm not afraid of her. I shouldn't have..." But she cut herself off.

"You shouldn't have listened to me." He'd finally spent enough time with Cindira to train his predictive speech patterns algorithms. "I know it could not have been easy, facing the woman who admitted to murdering your mother without tipping your hand, but it was necessary. If you make yourself an enemy of Johanna Tieg right now, you'll draw away from her ability to protect your father. In weakening her, you'd only strengthen whomever is keeping Rex a prisoner. You must continue your charade and work with Tybor until they're brought down. And you must protect GAIA."

"Protect GAIA!" Cindira laughed as she slicked her hair off her forehead. "How can *I* protect GAIA?"

"Don't you want to?"

Her mouth gaped. "Of course, I do, but how? Even if I make myself a new avatar and hack in—or somehow trace the one that appeared as if by magic in The Kingdom — what can I really do there?"

"You can listen." The mouse jumped up onto the coffee table to be eye-to-eye with her. "Miss, since your mother died, you've been made to feel invisible and sidelined. Sent to boarding school, while your step-siblings were being loved in a house with your father, forced to work under Kaylie's direction at Tybor all while she took credit for your work and abused your talents for her own gain. You've experienced nothing but the disadvantages of not being seen."

Laporte pulled himself up to as much height as his tiny body would offer. "But now it's time to realize, if they never look your way, they never see you coming."

"You're saying keep the status quo."

"As far as they know it," Laporte clarified. "Cast out your roots under the ground, so when you break the soil, you're in too deep to be swept away."

"You know, for a programmed entity, you have a great grasp on metaphor." She sat up. "You're right, but I'm just one person versus the whole system. I'm really good at what I do, but how can that ever be enough?"

It was time. "You're not alone, miss. There are others inside the Tybor systems who are ready to help you. One saved you in the arena, and again during your encounter with Johanna, creating a buffer so you could escape."

"I thought that was you each time. You were there." Cindira shifted in place. "But if it wasn't you, then who was it?"

A mouse couldn't smile, but Laporte wasn't just any mouse. "Let's just call her your fairy godmother."

CITY OF CINDERS (THE CINDERELLA MATRIX #1)

©2018 KENDRAI MEEKS

Published by Tulipe Noire Press

All rights reserved. No part of this publication may be reproduced, stored in a retrieval system or transmitted in any form or by any means, electronic, mechanical, photocopying, recording or otherwise without the prior permission of the publisher or in accordance with the provisions of the Copyright, Designs and Patents Act 1988 or under the terms of any license permitting limited copying issued by the Copyright Licensing Agency.

Published by: Kendrai Meeks

Text Design by: The Last TK, with compliments to the resources made available from Draft2Digital.

Cover Design by: Deranged Doctor

Edited by: Rebecca Boucher

A message from Kendrai:

I really, really hope you enjoyed *City of Cinders*. It is so different from anything I've written before (not a single kiss in the book AT ALL! Don't worry if that's what you're looking for. Book two will have kissing.) As an indie author without the backing of a large publisher or huge marketing budget, my biggest career challenge is gaining visibility in this booming industry. As a reader, I hope the entertainment you got from reading the book encourages you to be part of Team Meeks, so that I can continue to bring future fairytale-inspired urban fantasy books to your bookshelves. Readers often ask me in what way they can help, and here are a few quick, easy things that, while small, are powerful:

- Leave a review. Whether that's on the venue where you purchased this book, on a community reader site like Reddit or Goodreads, or on a blog, every bit is appreciated.

- Tell a book friend. Recs are one of the main ways I discover new books, and hope you do too.

- Join my mail list. It will help you stay aware of new releases, events I'll be appearing at, and other news. Also, I tend to do a lot of giveaways. (You get your first such giveaway right after joining the list.)

- Join one of my reader groups. I keep up with readers on both Facebook and Goodreads.

- For advanced practitioners: offer a goat sacrifice to a pagan spirit. Note: I can't condone actual goat sacrifice, so in lieu of that, I'd advise Haagan-Dazs or Ben & Jerry's ice cream eaten to bring glory to the 1980s rock idol of your choice. (If you do do this, I need pictures people. PICTURES.)

Further information can be found at my website, www.kendraimeeks.com. I'm also on Twitter, Instagram, Facebook, Pinterest, and Reddit as Kendrai Meeks. If you like romances, you may be interested in some of the titles I've written as either Killian McRae or Mari K. Cicero. Or you may not. No biggie.

ACKNOWLEDGMENTS:

To my author buds who listen to me complain and keep me accountable to my own goals: the Merry Martones, Elizabeth Hunter, and Tom Hansen (whose name I always write as "Tome" before correcting it, though that seems totally appropriate for an author, am I right?)

To my editor, Rebecca, who modeled this block of misshaped clay into something that would not only hold water, but a variety of other liquids.

To my ARC team, who provided me feedback and support.

To my kids who continue to be understanding on the nights when we have to eat pizza. Yes, again.

To my (ex) bosses, who, after twenty years of employment, told me to go be a writer already, with their blessings.

To all my parents, biological and spiritual, who continue to support all that I do, by choice or by necessity.

BOOKOLOGY

The Hood Chronicles Series

Requited Hood
Reluctant Hood
Relinquished Hood
Ravening Hood

The Cinderella Matrix

Court of Discontent
City of Cinders

Romance written as Killian McRae

A Love by any Measure

Snapped

All my Exes die from Hexes Series

The Motion of the Potion
Once You Go Demon
Hex Goddess
When Spell Freezes Over
Hung by the Fireplace

Science Ficiton written as Killian McRae

12.21.12: The Vessel

New Adult Romance written as Mari K. Cicero
Complements

The Start-Up Bride